FAUST

By
Johann Wolfgang von Goethe

Black & White Classics

ISBN: 978-1503262140

FAUST

Preface

It is twenty years since I first determined to attempt the translation of Faust, in the original metres. At that time, although more than a score of English translations of the First Part, and three or four of the Second Part, were in existence, the experiment had not yet been made. The prose version of Hayward seemed to have been accepted as the standard, in default of anything more satisfactory: the English critics, generally sustaining the translator in his views concerning the secondary importance of form in Poetry, practically discouraged any further attempt; and no one, familiar with rhythmical expression through the needs of his own nature, had devoted the necessary love and patience to an adequate reproduction of the great work of Goethe's life.

Mr. Brooks was the first to undertake the task, and the publication of his translation of the First Part (in 1856) induced me, for a time, to give up my own design. No previous English version exhibited such abnegation of the translator's own tastes and habits of thought, such reverent desire to present the original in its purest form. The care and conscience with which the work had been performed were so apparent, that I now state with reluctance what then seemed to me to be its only deficiencies,—a lack of the lyrical fire and fluency of the original in some passages, and an occasional lowering of the tone through the use of words which are literal, but not equivalent. The plan of translation adopted by Mr. Brooks was so entirely my own, that when further residence in Germany and a more careful study of both parts of Faust had satisfied me that the field was still open,—that the means furnished by the poetical affinity of the two languages had not yet been exhausted,—nothing remained for me but to follow him in all essential particulars. His example confirmed me in the belief that there were few difficulties in the way of a nearly literal yet thoroughly rhythmical version of Faust, which might not be overcome by loving labor. A comparison of seventeen English translations, in the arbitrary metres adopted by the translators, sufficiently showed the danger of allowing license in this respect: the white light of Goethe's thought was thereby passed through the tinted glass of other minds, and assumed the coloring of each. Moreover, the plea of selecting different metres in the hope of producing a similar effect is unreasonable, where the identical metres are possible.

The value of form, in a poetical work, is the first question to be considered. No poet ever understood this question more thoroughly than Goethe himself, or expressed a more positive opinion in regard to it. The alternative modes of translation which he presents (reported by Riemer, quoted by Mrs. Austin, in her "Characteristics of Goethe," and accepted by Mr. Hayward),[A] are quite independent of his views concerning the value of form, which we find given elsewhere, in the clearest and most emphatic manner.[B] Poetry is not simply a

3

fashion of expression: it is the form of expression absolutely required by a certain class of ideas. Poetry, indeed, may be distinguished from Prose by the single circumstance, that it is the utterance of whatever in man cannot be perfectly uttered in any other than a rhythmical form: it is useless to say that the naked meaning is independent of the form: on the contrary, the form contributes essentially to the fullness of the meaning. In Poetry which endures through its own inherent vitality, there is no forced union of these two elements. They are as intimately blended, and with the same mysterious beauty, as the sexes in the ancient Hermaphroditus. To attempt to represent Poetry in Prose, is very much like attempting to translate music into speech.[C]

[A] "'There are two maxims of translation,' says he: 'the one requires that the author, of a foreign nation, be brought to us in such a manner that we may regard him as our own; the other, on the contrary, demands of us that we transport ourselves over to him, and adopt his situation, his mode of speaking, and his peculiarities. The advantages of both are sufficiently known to all instructed persons, from masterly examples.'" Is it necessary, however, that there should always be this alternative? Where the languages are kindred, and equally capable of all varieties of metrical expression, may not both these "maxims" be observed in the same translation? Goethe, it is true, was of the opinion that Faust ought to be given, in French, in the manner of Clement Marot; but this was undoubtedly because he felt the inadequacy of modern French to express the naive, simple realism of many passages. The same objection does not apply to English. There are a few archaic expressions in Faust, but no more than are still allowed—nay, frequently encouraged—in the English of our day.

[B] "You are right," said Goethe; "there are great and mysterious agencies included in the various forms of Poetry. If the substance of my 'Roman Elegies' were to be expressed in the tone and measure of Byron's 'Don Juan,' it would really have an atrocious effect."—Eckermann.

"The rhythm," said Goethe, "is an unconscious result of the poetic mood. If one should stop to consider it mechanically, when about to write a poem, one would become bewildered and accomplish nothing of real poetical value."—Ibid.

"All that is poetic in character should be rythmically treated! Such is my conviction; and if even a sort of poetic prose should be gradually introduced, it would only show that the distinction between prose and poetry had been completely lost sight of."—Goethe to Schiller, 1797.

Tycho Mommsen, in his excellent essay, Die Kunst des Deutschen Uebersetzers aus neueren Sprachen, goes so far as to say: "The metrical or rhymed modelling of a poetical work is so essentially the germ of its being, that, rather than by giving it up, we might hope to construct a similar work of art before the eyes of our countrymen, by giving up or changing the substance. The immeasurable result which has followed works wherein the form has been retained—such as the Homer of Voss, and the Shakespeare of Tieck and Schlegel—is an incontrovertible evidence of the vitality of the endeavor."

[C] "Goethe's poems exercise a great sway over me, not only by their meaning, but also by their rhythm. It is a language which stimulates me to composition."—Beethoven.

The various theories of translation from the Greek and Latin poets have been admirably stated by Dryden in his Preface to the "Translations from Ovid's Epistles," and I do not wish to continue the endless discussion,—especially as our literature needs examples, not opinions. A recent expression, however, carries with it so much authority, that I feel bound to present some considerations which the accomplished scholar seems to have overlooked. Mr. Lewes[D] justly says: "The effect of poetry is a compound of music and suggestion; this music and this suggestion are intermingled in words, which to alter is to alter the effect. For words in poetry are not, as in prose, simple representatives of objects and ideas: they are parts of an organic whole,—they are tones in the harmony." He thereupon illustrates the effect of translation by changing certain well-known English stanzas into others, equivalent in meaning, but lacking their felicity of words, their grace and melody. I cannot accept this illustration as valid, because Mr. Lewes purposely omits the very quality which an honest translator should exhaust his skill in endeavoring to reproduce. He turns away from the one best word or phrase in the English lines he quotes, whereas the translator seeks precisely that one best word or phrase (having all the resources of his language at command), to represent what is said in another language. More than this, his task is not simply mechanical: he must feel, and be guided by, a secondary inspiration. Surrendering himself to the full possession of the spirit which shall speak through him, he receives, also, a portion of the same creative power. Mr. Lewes reaches this conclusion: "If, therefore, we reflect what a poem Faust is, and that it contains almost every variety of style and metre, it will be tolerably evident that no one unacquainted with the original can form an adequate idea of it from translation,"[E] which is certainly correct of any translation wherein something of the rhythmical variety and beauty of the original is not retained. That very much of the rhythmical character may be retained in English, was long ago shown by Mr. Carlyle,[F] in the passages which he translated, both literally and rhythmically, from the Helena (Part Second). In fact, we have so many instances of the possibility of reciprocally transferring the finest qualities of English and German poetry, that there is no sufficient excuse for an unmetrical translation of Faust. I refer especially to such subtile and melodious lyrics as "The Castle by the Sea," of Uhland, and the "Silent Land" of Salis, translated by Mr. Longfellow; Goethe's "Minstrel" and "Coptic Song," by Dr. Hedge; Heine's "Two Grenadiers," by Dr. Furness and many of Heine's songs by Mr Leland; and also to the German translations of English lyrics, by Freiligrath and Strodtmann.[G]

[D] Life of Goethe (Book VI.).

[E] Mr. Lewes gives the following advice: "The English reader would perhaps best succeed who should first read Dr. Anster's brilliant paraphrase, and then carefully go through Hayward's prose translation." This is singularly at variance

5

with the view he has just expressed. Dr. Anster's version is an almost incredible dilution of the original, written in other metres; while Hayward's entirely omits the element of poetry.

[F] Foreign Review, 1828.

[G] When Freiligrath can thus give us Walter Scott:—

"Kommt, wie der Wind kommt,
Wenn Wälder erzittern
Kommt, wie die Brandung
Wenn Flotten zersplittern!
Schnell heran, schnell herab,
Schneller kommt Al'e!—
Häuptling und Bub' und Knapp,
Herr und Vasalle!"

or Strodtmann thus reproduce Tennyson:—

"Es fällt der Strahl auf Burg und Thal,
Und schneeige Gipfel, reich an Sagen;
Viel' Lichter wehn auf blauen Seen,
Bergab die Wasserstürze jagen!
Blas, Hüfthorn, blas, in Wiederhall erschallend:
Blas, Horn—antwortet, Echos, hallend, hallend, hallend!"

—it must be a dull ear which would be satisfied with the omission of rhythm and rhyme.

I have a more serious objection, however, to urge against Mr. Hayward's prose translation. Where all the restraints of verse are flung aside, we should expect, at least, as accurate a reproduction of the sense, spirit, and tone of the original, as the genius of our language will permit. So far from having given us such a reproduction, Mr. Hayward not only occasionally mistakes the exact meaning of the German text,[H] but, wherever two phrases may be used to express the meaning with equal fidelity, he very frequently selects that which has the less grace, strength, or beauty.[I]

[H] On his second page, the line Mein Lied ertönt der unbekannten Menge, "My song sounds to the unknown multitude," is translated: "My sorrow voices itself to the strange throng." Other English translators, I notice, have followed Mr. Hayward in mistaking Lied for Leid.

[I] I take but one out of numerous instances, for the sake of illustration. The close of the Soldier's Song (Part I. Scene II.) is:—

"Kühn is das Mühen,
Herrlich der Lohn!
Und die Soldaten

Ziehen davon."

Literally:

Bold is the endeavor,
Splendid the pay!
And the soldiers
March away.

This Mr. Hayward translates:—

Bold the adventure,
Noble the reward—
And the soldiers
Are off.

For there are few things which may not be said, in English, in a twofold manner,—one poetic, and the other prosaic. In German, equally, a word which in ordinary use has a bare prosaic character may receive a fairer and finer quality from its place in verse. The prose translator should certainly be able to feel the manifestation of this law in both languages, and should so choose his words as to meet their reciprocal requirements. A man, however, who is not keenly sensible to the power and beauty and value of rhythm, is likely to overlook these delicate yet most necessary distinctions. The author's thought is stripped of a last grace in passing through his mind, and frequently presents very much the same resemblance to the original as an unhewn shaft to the fluted column. Mr. Hayward unconsciously illustrates his lack of a refined appreciation of verse, "in giving," as he says, "a sort of rhythmical arrangement to the lyrical parts," his object being "to convey some notion of the variety of versification which forms one great charm of the poem." A literal translation is always possible in the unrhymed passages; but even here Mr. Hayward's ear did not dictate to him the necessity of preserving the original rhythm.

While, therefore, I heartily recognize his lofty appreciation of Faust,—while I honor him for the patient and conscientious labor he has bestowed upon his translation,—I cannot but feel that he has himself illustrated the unsoundness of his argument. Nevertheless, the circumstance that his prose translation of Faust has received so much acceptance proves those qualities of the original work which cannot be destroyed by a test so violent. From the cold bare outline thus produced, the reader unacquainted with the German language would scarcely guess what glow of color, what richness of changeful life, what fluent grace and energy of movement have been lost in the process. We must, of course, gratefully receive such an outline, where a nearer approach to the form of the original is impossible, but, until the latter has been demonstrated, we are wrong to remain content with the cheaper substitute.

7

It seems to me that in all discussions upon this subject the capacities of the English language have received but scanty justice. The intellectual tendencies of our race have always been somewhat conservative, and its standards of literary taste or belief, once set up, are not varied without a struggle. The English ear is suspicious of new metres and unaccustomed forms of expression: there are critical detectives on the track of every author, and a violation of the accepted canons is followed by a summons to judgment. Thus the tendency is to contract rather than to expand the acknowledged excellences of the language.

[J] I cannot resist the temptation of quoting the following passage from Jacob Grimm: "No one of all the modern languages has acquired a greater force and strength than the English, through the derangement and relinquishment of its ancient laws of sound. The unteachable (nevertheless learnable) profusion of its middle-tones has conferred upon it an intrinsic power of expression, such as no other human tongue ever possessed. Its entire, thoroughly intellectual and wonderfully successful foundation and perfected development issued from a marvelous union of the two noblest tongues of Europe, the Germanic and the Romanic. Their mutual relation in the English language is well known, since the former furnished chiefly the material basis, while the latter added the intellectual conceptions. The English language, by and through which the greatest and most eminent poet of modern times—as contrasted with ancient classical poetry—(of course I can refer only to Shakespeare) was begotten and nourished, has a just claim to be called a language of the world; and it appears to be destined, like the English race, to a higher and broader sway in all quarters of the earth. For in richness, in compact adjustment of parts, and in pure intelligence, none of the living languages can be compared with it,—not even our German, which is divided even as we are divided, and which must cast off many imperfections before it can boldly enter on its career."—Ueber den Ursprung der Sprache.

The difficulties in the way of a nearly literal translation of Faust in the original metres have been exaggerated, because certain affinities between the two languages have not been properly considered. With all the splendor of versification in the work, it contains but few metres of which the English tongue is not equally capable. Hood has familiarized us with dactylic (triple) rhymes, and they are remarkably abundant and skillful in Mr. Lowell's "Fable for the Critics": even the unrhymed iambic hexameter of the Helena occurs now and then in Milton's Samson Agonistes. It is true that the metrical foot into which the German language most naturally falls is the trochaic, while in English it is the iambic: it is true that German is rich, involved, and tolerant of new combinations, while English is simple, direct, and rather shy of compounds; but precisely these differences are so modified in the German of Faust that there is a mutual approach of the two languages. In Faust, the iambic measure predominates; the style is compact; the many licenses which the author allows himself are all directed towards a shorter mode of construction. On the other hand, English metre compels the use of inversions, admits many verbal liberties prohibited to prose, and so inclines towards various flexible features of its sister-tongue that many lines of Faust may be repeated in English without the slightest change of meaning, measure, or rhyme. There are words, it is true, with so delicate a bloom upon them that it can in no wise be preserved; but even such words will always lose less when they carry with them their rhythmical atmosphere. The flow of Goethe's verse is sometimes so similar to that of the corresponding English metre, that not only its harmonies and caesural pauses, but even its punctuation, may be easily retained.

I am satisfied that the difference between a translation of Faust in prose or metre is chiefly one of labor,—and of that labor which is successful in proportion as it is joyously performed. My own task has been cheered by the discovery, that the more closely I reproduced the language of the original, the more of its rhythmical character was transferred at the same time. If, now and then, there was an inevitable alternative of meaning or music, I gave the preference to the former. By the term "original metres" I do not mean a rigid, unyielding adherence to every foot, line, and rhyme of the German original, although this has very nearly been accomplished. Since the greater part of the work is written in an irregular measure, the lines varying from three to six feet, and the rhymes arranged according to the author's will, I do not consider that an occasional change in the number of feet, or order of rhyme, is any violation of the metrical plan. The single slight liberty I have taken with the lyrical passages is in Margaret's song,—"The King of Thule,"—in which, by omitting the alternate feminine rhymes, yet retaining the metre, I was enabled to make the translation strictly literal. If, in two or three instances, I have left a line unrhymed, I have balanced the omission by giving rhymes to other lines which stand unrhymed in the original text. For the same reason, I make no apology for the imperfect rhymes, which are frequently a translation as well as a necessity. With all its supreme qualities, Faust is far from being a technically perfect work.[K]

[K] "At present, everything runs in technical grooves, and the critical gentlemen begin to wrangle whether in a rhyme an s should correspond with an s and not with sz. If I were young and reckless enough, I would purposely offend all such technical caprices: I would use alliteration, assonance, false rhyme, just according to my own will or convenience—but, at the same time, I would attend to the main thing, and endeavor to say so many good things that every one would be attracted to read and remember them."—Goethe, in 1831.

The feminine and dactylic rhymes, which have been for the most part omitted by all metrical translators except Mr. Brooks, are indispensable. The characteristic tone of many passages would be nearly lost, without them. They give spirit and grace to the dialogue, point to the aphoristic portions (especially in the Second Part), and an ever-changing music to the lyrical passages. The English language, though not so rich as the German in such rhymes, is less deficient than is generally supposed. The difficulty to be overcome is one of construction rather than of the vocabulary. The present participle can only be used to a limited extent, on account of its weak termination, and the want of an accusative form to the noun also restricts the arrangement of words in English verse. I cannot

9

hope to have been always successful; but I have at least labored long and patiently, bearing constantly in mind not only the meaning of the original and the mechanical structure of the lines, but also that subtile and haunting music which seems to govern rhythm instead of being governed by it.

AN GOETHE

I

Erhabener Geist, im Geisterreich verloren!
Wo immer Deine lichte Wohnung sey,
Zum höh'ren Schaffen bist Du neugeboren,
Und singest dort die voll're Litanei.
Von jenem Streben das Du auserkoren,
Vom reinsten Aether, drin Du athmest frei,
O neige Dich zu gnädigem Erwiedern
Des letzten Wiederhalls von Deinen Liedern!

II

Den alten Musen die bestäubten Kronen
Nahmst Du, zu neuem Glanz, mit kühner Hand:
Du löst die Räthsel ältester Aeonen
Durch jüngeren Glauben, helleren Verstand,
Und machst, wo rege Menschengeister wohnen,
Die ganze Erde Dir zum Vaterland;
Und Deine Jünger sehn in Dir, verwundert,
Verkörpert schon das werdende Jahrhundert.

III

Was Du gesungen, Aller Lust und Klagen,
Des Lebens Wiedersprüche, neu vermählt,—
Die Harfe tausendstimmig frisch geschlagen,
Die Shakspeare einst, die einst Homer gewählt,—
Darf ich in fremde Klänge übertragen
Das Alles, wo so Mancher schon gefehlt?
Lass Deinen Geist in meiner Stimme klingen,
Und was Du sangst, lass mich es Dir nachsingen!

DEDICATION

Again ye come, ye hovering Forms! I find ye,
As early to my clouded sight ye shone!
Shall I attempt, this once, to seize and bind ye?
Still o'er my heart is that illusion thrown?
Ye crowd more near! Then, be the reign assigned ye,
And sway me from your misty, shadowy zone!
My bosom thrills, with youthful passion shaken,
From magic airs that round your march awaken.
Of joyous days ye bring the blissful vision;
The dear, familiar phantoms rise again,
And, like an old and half-extinct tradition,
First Love returns, with Friendship in his train.
Renewed is Pain: with mournful repetition
Life tracks his devious, labyrinthine chain,
And names the Good, whose cheating fortune tore them
From happy hours, and left me to deplore them.
They hear no longer these succeeding measures,
The souls, to whom my earliest songs I sang:
Dispersed the friendly troop, with all its pleasures,
And still, alas! the echoes first that rang!
I bring the unknown multitude my treasures;
Their very plaudits give my heart a pang,
And those beside, whose joy my Song so flattered,
If still they live, wide through the world are scattered.
And grasps me now a long-unwonted yearning
For that serene and solemn Spirit-Land:
My song, to faint Aeolian murmurs turning,
Sways like a harp-string by the breezes fanned.
I thrill and tremble; tear on tear is burning,
And the stern heart is tenderly unmanned.
What I possess, I see far distant lying,
And what I lost, grows real and undying.

PRELUDE AT THE THEATRE

MANAGER = DRAMATIC POET = MERRY-ANDREW

MANAGER

You two, who oft a helping hand
Have lent, in need and tribulation.
Come, let me know your expectation
Of this, our enterprise, in German land!
I wish the crowd to feel itself well treated,
Especially since it lives and lets me live;
The posts are set, the booth of boards completed.
And each awaits the banquet I shall give.
Already there, with curious eyebrows raised,
They sit sedate, and hope to be amazed.
I know how one the People's taste may flatter,
Yet here a huge embarrassment I feel:
What they're accustomed to, is no great matter,
But then, alas! they've read an awful deal.
How shall we plan, that all be fresh and new,—
Important matter, yet attractive too?
For 'tis my pleasure-to behold them surging,
When to our booth the current sets apace,
And with tremendous, oft-repeated urging,
Squeeze onward through the narrow gate of grace:
By daylight even, they push and cram in
To reach the seller's box, a fighting host,
And as for bread, around a baker's door, in famine,
To get a ticket break their necks almost.
This miracle alone can work the Poet
On men so various: now, my friend, pray show it.

POET

Speak not to me of yonder motley masses,
Whom but to see, puts out the fire of Song!
Hide from my view the surging crowd that passes,
And in its whirlpool forces us along!
No, lead me where some heavenly silence glasses
The purer joys that round the Poet throng,—
Where Love and Friendship still divinely fashion
The bonds that bless, the wreaths that crown his passion!
Ah, every utterance from the depths of feeling
The timid lips have stammeringly expressed,—
Now failing, now, perchance, success revealing,—

Gulps the wild Moment in its greedy breast;
Or oft, reluctant years its warrant sealing,
Its perfect stature stands at last confessed!
What dazzles, for the Moment spends its spirit:
What's genuine, shall Posterity inherit.

MERRY-ANDREW
Posterity! Don't name the word to me!
If I should choose to preach Posterity,
Where would you get contemporary fun?
That men will have it, there's no blinking:
A fine young fellow's presence, to my thinking,
Is something worth, to every one.
Who genially his nature can outpour,
Takes from the People's moods no irritation;
The wider circle he acquires, the more
Securely works his inspiration.
Then pluck up heart, and give us sterling coin!
Let Fancy be with her attendants fitted,—
Sense, Reason, Sentiment, and Passion join,—
But have a care, lest Folly be omitted!

MANAGER
Chiefly, enough of incident prepare!
They come to look, and they prefer to stare.
Reel off a host of threads before their faces,
So that they gape in stupid wonder: then
By sheer diffuseness you have won their graces,
And are, at once, most popular of men.
Only by mass you touch the mass; for any
Will finally, himself, his bit select:
Who offers much, brings something unto many,
And each goes home content with the effect,
If you've a piece, why, just in pieces give it:
A hash, a stew, will bring success, believe it!
'Tis easily displayed, and easy to invent.
What use, a Whole compactly to present?
Your hearers pick and pluck, as soon as they receive it!

POET
You do not feel, how such a trade debases;
How ill it suits the Artist, proud and true!
The botching work each fine pretender traces
Is, I perceive, a principle with you.

14

MANAGER

Such a reproach not in the least offends;
A man who some result intends
Must use the tools that best are fitting.
Reflect, soft wood is given to you for splitting,
And then, observe for whom you write!
If one comes bored, exhausted quite,
Another, satiate, leaves the banquet's tapers,
And, worst of all, full many a wight
Is fresh from reading of the daily papers.
Idly to us they come, as to a masquerade,
Mere curiosity their spirits warming:
The ladies with themselves, and with their finery, aid,
Without a salary their parts performing.
What dreams are yours in high poetic places?
You're pleased, forsooth, full houses to behold?
Draw near, and view your patrons' faces!
The half are coarse, the half are cold.
One, when the play is out, goes home to cards;
A wild night on a wench's breast another chooses:
Why should you rack, poor, foolish bards,
For ends like these, the gracious Muses?
I tell you, give but more—more, ever more, they ask:
Thus shall you hit the mark of gain and glory.
Seek to confound your auditory!
To satisfy them is a task.—
What ails you now? Is't suffering, or pleasure?

POET

Go, find yourself a more obedient slave!
What! shall the Poet that which Nature gave,
The highest right, supreme Humanity,
Forfeit so wantonly, to swell your treasure?
Whence o'er the heart his empire free?
The elements of Life how conquers he?
Is't not his heart's accord, urged outward far and dim,
To wind the world in unison with him?
When on the spindle, spun to endless distance,
By Nature's listless hand the thread is twirled,
And the discordant tones of all existence
In sullen jangle are together hurled,
Who, then, the changeless orders of creation
Divides, and kindles into rhythmic dance?

15

Who brings the One to join the general ordination,
Where it may throb in grandest consonance?
Who bids the storm to passion stir the bosom?
In brooding souls the sunset burn above?
Who scatters every fairest April blossom
Along the shining path of Love?
Who braids the noteless leaves to crowns, requiting
Desert with fame, in Action's every field?
Who makes Olympus sure, the Gods uniting?
The might of Man, as in the Bard revealed.

MERRY-ANDREW
So, these fine forces, in conjunction,
Propel the high poetic function,
As in a love-adventure they might play!
You meet by accident; you feel, you stay,
And by degrees your heart is tangled;
Bliss grows apace, and then its course is jangled;
You're ravished quite, then comes a touch of woe,
And there's a neat romance, completed ere you know!
Let us, then, such a drama give!
Grasp the exhaustless life that all men live!
Each shares therein, though few may comprehend:
Where'er you touch, there's interest without end.
In motley pictures little light,
Much error, and of truth a glimmering mite,
Thus the best beverage is supplied,
Whence all the world is cheered and edified.
Then, at your play, behold the fairest flower
Of youth collect, to hear the revelation!
Each tender soul, with sentimental power,
Sucks melancholy food from your creation;
And now in this, now that, the leaven works.
For each beholds what in his bosom lurks.
They still are moved at once to weeping or to laughter,
Still wonder at your flights, enjoy the show they see:
A mind, once formed, is never suited after;
One yet in growth will ever grateful be.

POET
Then give me back that time of pleasures,
While yet in joyous growth I sang,—
When, like a fount, the crowding measures
Uninterrupted gushed and sprang!

Then bright mist veiled the world before me,
In opening buds a marvel woke,
As I the thousand blossoms broke,
Which every valley richly bore me!
I nothing had, and yet enough for youth—
Joy in Illusion, ardent thirst for Truth.
Give, unrestrained, the old emotion,
The bliss that touched the verge of pain,
The strength of Hate, Love's deep devotion,—
O, give me back my youth again!

MERRY ANDREW

Youth, good my friend, you certainly require
When foes in combat sorely press you;
When lovely maids, in fond desire,
Hang on your bosom and caress you;
When from the hard-won goal the wreath
Beckons afar, the race awaiting;
When, after dancing out your breath,
You pass the night in dissipating:—
But that familiar harp with soul
To play,—with grace and bold expression,
And towards a self-erected goal
To walk with many a sweet digression,—
This, aged Sirs, belongs to you,
And we no less revere you for that reason:
Age childish makes, they say, but 'tis not true;
We're only genuine children still, in Age's season!

MANAGER

The words you've bandied are sufficient;
'Tis deeds that I prefer to see:
In compliments you're both proficient,
But might, the while, more useful be.
What need to talk of Inspiration?
'Tis no companion of Delay.
If Poetry be your vocation,
Let Poetry your will obey!
Full well you know what here is wanting;
The crowd for strongest drink is panting,
And such, forthwith, I'd have you brew.
What's left undone to-day, To-morrow will not do.
Waste not a day in vain digression:
With resolute, courageous trust

Seize every possible impression,
And make it firmly your possession;
You'll then work on, because you must.
Upon our German stage, you know it,
Each tries his hand at what he will;
So, take of traps and scenes your fill,
And all you find, be sure to show it!
Use both the great and lesser heavenly light,—
Squander the stars in any number,
Beasts, birds, trees, rocks, and all such lumber,
Fire, water, darkness, Day and Night!
Thus, in our booth's contracted sphere,
The circle of Creation will appear,
And move, as we deliberately impel,
From Heaven, across the World, to Hell!

PROLOGUE IN HEAVEN

THE LORD = THE HEAVENLY HOST
Afterwards
MEPHISTOPHELES
(The THREE ARCHANGELS come forward.)

RAPHAEL

The sun-orb sings, in emulation,
'Mid brother-spheres, his ancient round:
His path predestined through Creation
He ends with step of thunder-sound.
The angels from his visage splendid
Draw power, whose measure none can say;
The lofty works, uncomprehended,
Are bright as on the earliest day.

GABRIEL

And swift, and swift beyond conceiving,
The splendor of the world goes round,
Day's Eden-brightness still relieving
The awful Night's intense profound:
The ocean-tides in foam are breaking,
Against the rocks' deep bases hurled,
And both, the spheric race partaking,
Eternal, swift, are onward whirled!

MICHAEL

And rival storms abroad are surging
From sea to land, from land to sea.
A chain of deepest action forging
Round all, in wrathful energy.
There flames a desolation, blazing
Before the Thunder's crashing way:
Yet, Lord, Thy messengers are praising
The gentle movement of Thy Day.

THE THREE

Though still by them uncomprehended,
From these the angels draw their power,
And all Thy works, sublime and splendid,
Are bright as in Creation's hour.

MEPHISTOPHELES

19

Since Thou, O Lord, deign'st to approach again
And ask us how we do, in manner kindest,
And heretofore to meet myself wert fain,
Among Thy menials, now, my face Thou findest.
Pardon, this troop I cannot follow after
With lofty speech, though by them scorned and spurned:
My pathos certainly would move Thy laughter,
If Thou hadst not all merriment unlearned.
Of suns and worlds I've nothing to be quoted;
How men torment themselves, is all I've noted.
The little god o' the world sticks to the same old way,
And is as whimsical as on Creation's day.
Life somewhat better might content him,
But for the gleam of heavenly light which Thou hast lent
him:
He calls it Reason—thence his power's increased,
To be far beastlier than any beast.
Saving Thy Gracious Presence, he to me
A long-legged grasshopper appears to be,
That springing flies, and flying springs,
And in the grass the same old ditty sings.
Would he still lay among the grass he grows in!
Each bit of dung he seeks, to stick his nose in.

THE LORD
Hast thou, then, nothing more to mention?
Com'st ever, thus, with ill intention?
Find'st nothing right on earth, eternally?

MEPHISTOPHELES
No, Lord! I find things, there, still bad as they can be.
Man's misery even to pity moves my nature;
I've scarce the heart to plague the wretched creature.

THE LORD
Know'st Faust?

MEPHISTOPHELES
The Doctor Faust?

THE LORD
My servant, he!

MEPHISTOPHELES

Forsooth! He serves you after strange devices:
No earthly meat or drink the fool suffices:
His spirit's ferment far aspireth;
Half conscious of his frenzied, crazed unrest,
The fairest stars from Heaven he requireth,
From Earth the highest raptures and the best,
And all the Near and Far that he desireth
Fails to subdue the tumult of his breast.

THE LORD
Though still confused his service unto Me,
I soon shall lead him to a clearer morning.
Sees not the gardener, even while buds his tree,
Both flower and fruit the future years adorning?

MEPHISTOPHELES
What will you bet? There's still a chance to gain him,
If unto me full leave you give,
Gently upon my road to train him!

THE LORD
As long as he on earth shall live,
So long I make no prohibition.
While Man's desires and aspirations stir,
He cannot choose but err.

MEPHISTOPHELES
My thanks! I find the dead no acquisition,
And never cared to have them in my keeping.
I much prefer the cheeks where ruddy blood is leaping,
And when a corpse approaches, close my house:
It goes with me, as with the cat the mouse.

THE LORD
Enough! What thou hast asked is granted.
Turn off this spirit from his fountain-head;
To trap him, let thy snares be planted,
And him, with thee, be downward led;
Then stand abashed, when thou art forced to say:
A good man, through obscurest aspiration,
Has still an instinct of the one true way.

MEPHISTOPHELES
Agreed! But 'tis a short probation.

About my bet I feel no trepidation.
If I fulfill my expectation,
You'll let me triumph with a swelling breast:
Dust shall he eat, and with a zest,
As did a certain snake, my near relation.

THE LORD
Therein thou'rt free, according to thy merits;
The like of thee have never moved My hate.
Of all the bold, denying Spirits,
The waggish knave least trouble doth create.
Man's active nature, flagging, seeks too soon the level;
Unqualified repose he learns to crave;
Whence, willingly, the comrade him I gave,
Who works, excites, and must create, as Devil.
But ye, God's sons in love and duty,
Enjoy the rich, the ever-living Beauty!
Creative Power, that works eternal schemes,
Clasp you in bonds of love, relaxing never,
And what in wavering apparition gleams
Fix in its place with thoughts that stand forever!

(Heaven closes: the ARCHANGELS separate.)

MEPHISTOPHELES (solus)
I like, at times, to hear The Ancient's word,
And have a care to be most civil:
It's really kind of such a noble Lord
So humanly to gossip with the Devil!

FIRST PART OF THE TRAGEDY
I
NIGHT

(A lofty-arched, narrow, Gothic chamber. FAUST, in a chair at his desk, restless.)

FAUST

I've studied now Philosophy
And Jurisprudence, Medicine,—
And even, alas! Theology,—
From end to end, with labor keen;
And here, poor fool! with all my lore
I stand, no wiser than before:
I'm Magister—yea, Doctor—hight,
And straight or cross-wise, wrong or right,
These ten years long, with many woes,
I've led my scholars by the nose,—
And see, that nothing can be known!
That knowledge cuts me to the bone.
I'm cleverer, true, than those fops of teachers,
Doctors and Magisters, Scribes and Preachers;
Neither scruples nor doubts come now to smite me,
Nor Hell nor Devil can longer affright me.
For this, all pleasure am I foregoing;
I do not pretend to aught worth knowing,
I do not pretend I could be a teacher
To help or convert a fellow-creature.
Then, too, I've neither lands nor gold,
Nor the world's least pomp or honor hold—
No dog would endure such a curst existence!
Wherefore, from Magic I seek assistance,
That many a secret perchance I reach
Through spirit-power and spirit-speech,
And thus the bitter task forego
Of saying the things I do not know,—
That I may detect the inmost force
Which binds the world, and guides its course;
Its germs, productive powers explore,
And rummage in empty words no more!
O full and splendid Moon, whom I
Have, from this desk, seen climb the sky
So many a midnight,—would thy glow
For the last time beheld my woe!
Ever thine eye, most mournful friend,

23

O'er books and papers saw me bend;
But would that I, on mountains grand,
Amid thy blessed light could stand,
With spirits through mountain-caverns hover,
Float in thy twilight the meadows over,
And, freed from the fumes of lore that swathe me,
To health in thy dewy fountains bathe me!
Ah, me! this dungeon still I see.
This drear, accursed masonry,
Where even the welcome daylight strains
But duskly through the painted panes.
Hemmed in by many a toppling heap
Of books worm-eaten, gray with dust,
Which to the vaulted ceiling creep,
Against the smoky paper thrust,—
With glasses, boxes, round me stacked,
And instruments together hurled,
Ancestral lumber, stuffed and packed—
Such is my world: and what a world!
And do I ask, wherefore my heart
Falters, oppressed with unknown needs?
Why some inexplicable smart
All movement of my life impedes?
Alas! in living Nature's stead,
Where God His human creature set,
In smoke and mould the fleshless dead
And bones of beasts surround me yet!
Fly! Up, and seek the broad, free land!
And this one Book of Mystery
From Nostradamus' very hand,
Is't not sufficient company?
When I the starry courses know,
And Nature's wise instruction seek,
With light of power my soul shall glow,
As when to spirits spirits speak.
Tis vain, this empty brooding here,
Though guessed the holy symbols be:
Ye, Spirits, come—ye hover near—
Oh, if you hear me, answer me!
(He opens the Book, and perceives the sign of the Macrocosm.)
Ha! what a sudden rapture leaps from this
I view, through all my senses swiftly flowing!
I feel a youthful, holy, vital bliss
In every vein and fibre newly glowing.

Was it a God, who traced this sign,
With calm across my tumult stealing,
My troubled heart to joy unsealing,
With impulse, mystic and divine,
The powers of Nature here, around my path, revealing?
Am I a God?—so clear mine eyes!
In these pure features I behold
Creative Nature to my soul unfold.
What says the sage, now first I recognize:
"The spirit-world no closures fasten;
Thy sense is shut, thy heart is dead:
Disciple, up! untiring, hasten
To bathe thy breast in morning-red!"
(He contemplates the sign.)
How each the Whole its substance gives,
Each in the other works and lives!
Like heavenly forces rising and descending,
Their golden urns reciprocally lending,
With wings that winnow blessing
From Heaven through Earth I see them pressing,
Filling the All with harmony unceasing!
How grand a show! but, ah! a show alone.
Thee, boundless Nature, how make thee my own?
Where you, ye beasts? Founts of all Being, shining,
Whereon hang Heaven's and Earth's desire,
Whereto our withered hearts aspire,—
Ye flow, ye feed: and am I vainly pining?
(He turns the leaves impatiently, and perceives the sign of the
Earth-Spirit.)
How otherwise upon me works this sign!
Thou, Spirit of the Earth, art nearer:
Even now my powers are loftier, clearer;
I glow, as drunk with new-made wine:
New strength and heart to meet the world incite me,
The woe of earth, the bliss of earth, invite me,
And though the shock of storms may smite me,
No crash of shipwreck shall have power to fright me!
Clouds gather over me—
The moon conceals her light—
The lamp's extinguished!—
Mists rise,—red, angry rays are darting
Around my head!—There falls
A horror from the vaulted roof,
And seizes me!

I feel thy presence, Spirit I invoke!
Reveal thyself!
Ha! in my heart what rending stroke!
With new impulsion
My senses heave in this convulsion!
I feel thee draw my heart, absorb, exhaust me:
Thou must! thou must! and though my life it cost me!
(He seizes the book, and mysteriously pronounces the sign of
the Spirit. A ruddy flame flashes: the Spirit appears in
the flame.)

SPIRIT
Who calls me?

FAUST (with averted head)
Terrible to see!
SPIRIT
Me hast thou long with might attracted,
Long from my sphere thy food exacted,
And now—

FAUST
Woe! I endure not thee!

SPIRIT
To view me is thine aspiration,
My voice to hear, my countenance to see;
Thy powerful yearning moveth me,
Here am I!—what mean perturbation
Thee, superhuman, shakes? Thy soul's high calling, where?
Where is the breast, which from itself a world did bear,
And shaped and cherished—which with joy expanded,
To be our peer, with us, the Spirits, banded?
Where art thou, Faust, whose voice has pierced to me,
Who towards me pressed with all thine energy?
He art thou, who, my presence breathing, seeing,
Trembles through all the depths of being,
A writhing worm, a terror-stricken form?

FAUST
Thee, form of flame, shall I then fear?
Yes, I am Faust: I am thy peer!

SPIRIT

In the tides of Life, in Action's storm,
A fluctuant wave,
A shuttle free,
Birth and the Grave,
An eternal sea,
A weaving, flowing
Life, all-glowing,
Thus at Time's humming loom 'tis my hand prepares
The garment of Life which the Deity wears!

FAUST
Thou, who around the wide world wendest,
Thou busy Spirit, how near I feel to thee!

SPIRIT
Thou'rt like the Spirit which thou comprehendest,
Not me!
(Disappears.)

FAUST (overwhelmed)
Not thee!
Whom then?
I, image of the Godhead!
Not even like thee!
(A knock).
O Death!—I know it—'tis my Famulus!
My fairest luck finds no fruition:
In all the fullness of my vision
The soulless sneak disturbs me thus!
(Enter WAGNER, in dressing-gown and night-cap, a lamp in
his hand. FAUST turns impatiently.)

WAGNER
Pardon, I heard your declamation;
'Twas sure an old Greek tragedy you read?
In such an art I crave some preparation,
Since now it stands one in good stead.
I've often heard it said, a preacher
Might learn, with a comedian for a teacher.

FAUST
Yes, when the priest comedian is by nature,
As haply now and then the case may be.

WAGNER

Ah, when one studies thus, a prisoned creature,
That scarce the world on holidays can see,—
Scarce through a glass, by rare occasion,
How shall one lead it by persuasion?

FAUST

You'll ne'er attain it, save you know the feeling,
Save from the soul it rises clear,
Serene in primal strength, compelling
The hearts and minds of all who hear.
You sit forever gluing, patching;
You cook the scraps from others' fare;
And from your heap of ashes hatching
A starveling flame, ye blow it bare!
Take children's, monkeys' gaze admiring,
If such your taste, and be content;
But ne'er from heart to heart you'll speak inspiring,
Save your own heart is eloquent!

WAGNER

Yet through delivery orators succeed;
I feel that I am far behind, indeed.

FAUST

Seek thou the honest recompense!
Beware, a tinkling fool to be!
With little art, clear wit and sense
Suggest their own delivery;
And if thou'rt moved to speak in earnest,
What need, that after words thou yearnest?
Yes, your discourses, with their glittering show,
Where ye for men twist shredded thought like paper,
Are unrefreshing as the winds that blow
The rustling leaves through chill autumnal vapor!

WAGNER

Ah, God! but Art is long,
And Life, alas! is fleeting.
And oft, with zeal my critic-duties meeting,
In head and breast there's something wrong.
How hard it is to compass the assistance
Whereby one rises to the source!
And, haply, ere one travels half the course

Must the poor devil quit existence.

FAUST

Is parchment, then, the holy fount before thee,
A draught wherefrom thy thirst forever slakes?
No true refreshment can restore thee,
Save what from thine own soul spontaneous breaks.

WAGNER

Pardon! a great delight is granted
When, in the spirit of the ages planted,
We mark how, ere our times, a sage has thought,
And then, how far his work, and grandly, we have brought.

FAUST

O yes, up to the stars at last!
Listen, my friend: the ages that are past
Are now a book with seven seals protected:
What you the Spirit of the Ages call
Is nothing but the spirit of you all,
Wherein the Ages are reflected.
So, oftentimes, you miserably mar it!
At the first glance who sees it runs away.
An offal-barrel and a lumber-garret,
Or, at the best, a Punch-and-Judy play,
With maxims most pragmatical and hitting,
As in the mouths of puppets are befitting!

WAGNER

But then, the world—the human heart and brain!
Of these one covets some slight apprehension.

FAUST

Yes, of the kind which men attain!
Who dares the child's true name in public mention?
The few, who thereof something really learned,
Unwisely frank, with hearts that spurned concealing,
And to the mob laid bare each thought and feeling,
Have evermore been crucified and burned.
I pray you, Friend, 'tis now the dead of night;
Our converse here must be suspended.

WAGNER

I would have shared your watches with delight,

That so our learned talk might be extended.
To-morrow, though, I'll ask, in Easter leisure,
This and the other question, at your pleasure.
Most zealously I seek for erudition:
Much do I know—but to know all is my ambition.
[Exit.

FAUST (solus)
That brain, alone, not loses hope, whose choice is
To stick in shallow trash forevermore,—
Which digs with eager hand for buried ore,
And, when it finds an angle-worm, rejoices!
Dare such a human voice disturb the flow,
Around me here, of spirit-presence fullest?
And yet, this once my thanks I owe
To thee, of all earth's sons the poorest, dullest!
For thou hast torn me from that desperate state
Which threatened soon to overwhelm my senses:
The apparition was so giant-great,
It dwarfed and withered all my soul's pretences!
I, image of the Godhead, who began—
Deeming Eternal Truth secure in nearness—
Ye choirs, have ye begun the sweet, consoling chant,
Which, through the night of Death, the angels ministrant
Sang, God's new Covenant repeating?

CHORUS OF WOMEN
With spices and precious
Balm, we arrayed him;
Faithful and gracious,
We tenderly laid him:
Linen to bind him
Cleanlily wound we:
Ah! when we would find him,
Christ no more found we!

CHORUS OF ANGELS
Christ is ascended!
Bliss hath invested him,—
Woes that molested him,
Trials that tested him,
Gloriously ended!

FAUST

Why, here in dust, entice me with your spell,
Ye gentle, powerful sounds of Heaven?
Peal rather there, where tender natures dwell.
Your messages I hear, but faith has not been given;
The dearest child of Faith is Miracle.
I venture not to soar to yonder regions
Whence the glad tidings hither float;
And yet, from childhood up familiar with the note,
To Life it now renews the old allegiance.
Once Heavenly Love sent down a burning kiss
Upon my brow, in Sabbath silence holy;
And, filled with mystic presage, chimed the church-bell slowly,
And prayer dissolved me in a fervent bliss.
A sweet, uncomprehended yearning
Drove forth my feet through woods and meadows free,
And while a thousand tears were burning,
I felt a world arise for me.
These chants, to youth and all its sports appealing,
Proclaimed the Spring's rejoicing holiday;
And Memory holds me now, with childish feeling,
Back from the last, the solemn way.
Sound on, ye hymns of Heaven, so sweet and mild!
My tears gush forth: the Earth takes back her child!

CHORUS OF DISCIPLES
Has He, victoriously,
Burst from the vaulted
Grave, and all-gloriously
Now sits exalted?
Is He, in glow of birth,
Rapture creative near?
Ah! to the woe of earth
Still are we native here.
We, his aspiring
Followers, Him we miss;
Weeping, desiring,
Master, Thy bliss!
CHORUS OF ANGELS
Christ is arisen,
Out of Corruption's womb:
Burst ye the prison,
Break from your gloom!
Praising and pleading him,
Lovingly needing him,

31

Brotherly feeding him,
Preaching and speeding him,
Blessing, succeeding Him,
Thus is the Master near,—
Thus is He here!

 Before the City-Gate

II
BEFORE THE CITY-GATE
(Pedestrians of all kinds come forth.)

SEVERAL APPRENTICES
Why do you go that way?
OTHERS
We're for the Hunters' lodge, to-day.
THE FIRST
We'll saunter to the Mill, in yonder hollow.
AN APPRENTICE
Go to the River Tavern, I should say.
SECOND APPRENTICE
But then, it's not a pleasant way.
THE OTHERS
And what will you?
A THIRD
As goes the crowd, I follow.
A FOURTH
Come up to Burgdorf? There you'll find good cheer,
The finest lasses and the best of beer,
And jolly rows and squabbles, trust me!
A FIFTH
You swaggering fellow, is your hide
A third time itching to be tried?
I won't go there, your jolly rows disgust me!
SERVANT-GIRL
No,—no! I'll turn and go to town again.
ANOTHER
We'll surely find him by those poplars yonder.
THE FIRST
That's no great luck for me, 'tis plain.
You'll have him, when and where you wander:
His partner in the dance you'll be,—
But what is all your fun to me?
THE OTHER
He's surely not alone to-day:
He'll be with Curly-head, I heard him say.
A STUDENT
Deuce! how they step, the buxom wenches!
Come, Brother! we must see them to the benches.
A strong, old beer, a pipe that stings and bites,
A girl in Sunday clothes,—these three are my delights.
CITIZEN'S DAUGHTER

Just see those handsome fellows, there!
It's really shameful, I declare;—
To follow servant-girls, when they
Might have the most genteel society to-day!
SECOND STUDENT (to the First)
Not quite so fast! Two others come behind,—
Those, dressed so prettily and neatly.
My neighbor's one of them, I find,
A girl that takes my heart, completely.
They go their way with looks demure,
But they'll accept us, after all, I'm sure.
THE FIRST
No, Brother! not for me their formal ways.
Quick! lest our game escape us in the press:
The hand that wields the broom on Saturdays
Will best, on Sundays, fondle and caress.
CITIZEN
He suits me not at all, our new-made Burgomaster!
Since he's installed, his arrogance grows faster.
How has he helped the town, I say?
Things worsen,—what improvement names he?
Obedience, more than ever, claims he,
And more than ever we must pay!
BEGGAR (sings)
Good gentlemen and lovely ladies,
So red of cheek and fine of dress,
Behold, how needful here your aid is,
And see and lighten my distress!
Let me not vainly sing my ditty;
He's only glad who gives away:
A holiday, that shows your pity,
Shall be for me a harvest-day!
ANOTHER CITIZEN
On Sundays, holidays, there's naught I take delight in,
Like gossiping of war, and war's array,
When down in Turkey, far away,
The foreign people are a-fighting.
One at the window sits, with glass and friends,
And sees all sorts of ships go down the river gliding:
And blesses then, as home he wends
At night, our times of peace abiding.
THIRD CITIZEN
Yes, Neighbor! that's my notion, too:
Why, let them break their heads, let loose their passions,

34

And mix things madly through and through,
So, here, we keep our good old fashions!
OLD WOMAN (to the Citizen's Daughter)
Dear me, how fine! So handsome, and so young!
Who wouldn't lose his heart, that met you?
Don't be so proud! I'll hold my tongue,
And what you'd like I'll undertake to get you.
CITIZEN'S DAUGHTER
Come, Agatha! I shun the witch's sight
Before folks, lest there be misgiving:
'Tis true, she showed me, on Saint Andrew's Night,
My future sweetheart, just as he were living.
THE OTHER
She showed me mine, in crystal clear,
With several wild young blades, a soldier-lover:
I seek him everywhere, I pry and peer,
And yet, somehow, his face I can't discover.
SOLDIERS
Castles, with lofty
Ramparts and towers,
Maidens disdainful
In Beauty's array,
Both shall be ours!
Bold is the venture,
Splendid the pay!
Lads, let the trumpets
For us be suing,—
Calling to pleasure,
Calling to ruin.
Stormy our life is;
Such is its boon!
Maidens and castles
Capitulate soon.
Bold is the venture,
Splendid the pay!
And the soldiers go marching,
Marching away!
FAUST AND WAGNER
FAUST
Released from ice are brook and river
By the quickening glance of the gracious Spring;
The colors of hope to the valley cling,
And weak old Winter himself must shiver,
Withdrawn to the mountains, a crownless king:

Whence, ever retreating, he sends again
Impotent showers of sleet that darkle
In belts across the green o' the plain.
But the sun will permit no white to sparkle;
Everywhere form in development moveth;
He will brighten the world with the tints he loveth,
And, lacking blossoms, blue, yellow, and red,
He takes these gaudy people instead.
Turn thee about, and from this height
Back on the town direct thy sight.
Out of the hollow, gloomy gate,
The motley throngs come forth elate:
Each will the joy of the sunshine hoard,
To honor the Day of the Risen Lord!
They feel, themselves, their resurrection:
From the low, dark rooms, scarce habitable;
From the bonds of Work, from Trade's restriction;
From the pressing weight of roof and gable;
From the narrow, crushing streets and alleys;
From the churches' solemn and reverend night,
All come forth to the cheerful light.
How lively, see! the multitude sallies,
Scattering through gardens and fields remote,
While over the river, that broadly dallies,
Dances so many a festive boat;
And overladen, nigh to sinking,
The last full wherry takes the stream.
Yonder afar, from the hill-paths blinking,
Their clothes are colors that softly gleam.
I hear the noise of the village, even;
Here is the People's proper Heaven;
Here high and low contented see!
Here I am Man,—dare man to be!
WAGNER
To stroll with you, Sir Doctor, flatters;
'Tis honor, profit, unto me.
But I, alone, would shun these shallow matters,
Since all that's coarse provokes my enmity.
This fiddling, shouting, ten-pin rolling
I hate,—these noises of the throng:
They rave, as Satan were their sports controlling,
And call it mirth, and call it song!
PEASANTS, UNDER THE LINDEN-TREE
(Dance and Song.)

All for the dance the shepherd dressed,
In ribbons, wreath, and gayest vest
Himself with care arraying:
Around the linden lass and lad
Already footed it like mad:
Hurrah! hurrah!
Hurrah—tarara-la!
The fiddle-bow was playing.
He broke the ranks, no whit afraid,
And with his elbow punched a maid,
Who stood, the dance surveying:
The buxom wench, she turned and said:
"Now, you I call a stupid-head!"
Hurrah! hurrah!
Hurrah—tarara-la!
"Be decent while you're staying!"
Then round the circle went their flight,
They danced to left, they danced to right:
Their kirtles all were playing.
They first grew red, and then grew warm,
And rested, panting, arm in arm,—
Hurrah! hurrah!
Hurrah—tarara-la!
And hips and elbows straying.
Now, don't be so familiar here!
How many a one has fooled his dear,
Waylaying and betraying!
And yet, he coaxed her soon aside,
And round the linden sounded wide.
Hurrah! hurrah!
Hurrah—tarara-la!
And the fiddle-bow was playing.
OLD PEASANT
Sir Doctor, it is good of you,
That thus you condescend, to-day,
Among this crowd of merry folk,
A highly-learned man, to stray.
Then also take the finest can,
We fill with fresh wine, for your sake:
I offer it, and humbly wish
That not alone your thirst is slake,—
That, as the drops below its brink,
So many days of life you drink!
FAUST

I take the cup you kindly reach,
With thanks and health to all and each.
(The People gather in a circle about him.)
OLD PEASANT
In truth, 'tis well and fitly timed,
That now our day of joy you share,
Who heretofore, in evil days,
Gave us so much of helping care.
Still many a man stands living here,
Saved by your father's skillful hand,
That snatched him from the fever's rage
And stayed the plague in all the land.
Then also you, though but a youth,
Went into every house of pain:
Many the corpses carried forth,
But you in health came out again.
FAUST
No test or trial you evaded:
A Helping God the helper aided.
ALL
Health to the man, so skilled and tried.
That for our help he long may abide!
FAUST
To Him above bow down, my friends,
Who teaches help, and succor sends!
(He goes on with WAGNER.)
WAGNER
With what a feeling, thou great man, must thou
Receive the people's honest veneration!
How lucky he, whose gifts his station
With such advantages endow!
Thou'rt shown to all the younger generation:
Each asks, and presses near to gaze;
The fiddle stops, the dance delays.
Thou goest, they stand in rows to see,
And all the caps are lifted high;
A little more, and they would bend the knee
As if the Holy Host came by.
FAUST
A few more steps ascend, as far as yonder stone!—
Here from our wandering will we rest contented.
Here, lost in thought, I've lingered oft alone,
When foolish fasts and prayers my life tormented.
Here, rich in hope and firm in faith,

38

With tears, wrung hands and sighs, I've striven,
The end of that far-spreading death
Entreating from the Lord of Heaven!
Now like contempt the crowd's applauses seem:
Couldst thou but read, within mine inmost spirit,
How little now I deem,
That sire or son such praises merit!
My father's was a sombre, brooding brain,
Which through the holy spheres of Nature groped and wandered,
And honestly, in his own fashion, pondered
With labor whimsical, and pain:
Who, in his dusky work-shop bending,
With proved adepts in company,
Made, from his recipes unending,
Opposing substances agree.
There was a Lion red, a wooer daring,
Within the Lily's tepid bath espoused,
And both, tormented then by flame unsparing,
By turns in either bridal chamber housed.
If then appeared, with colors splendid,
The young Queen in her crystal shell,
This was the medicine—the patients' woes soon ended,
And none demanded: who got well?
Thus we, our hellish boluses compounding,
Among these vales and hills surrounding,
Worse than the pestilence, have passed.
Thousands were done to death from poison of my giving;
And I must hear, by all the living,
The shameless murderers praised at last!

WAGNER

Why, therefore, yield to such depression?
A good man does his honest share
In exercising, with the strictest care,
The art bequeathed to his possession!
Dost thou thy father honor, as a youth?
Then may his teaching cheerfully impel thee:
Dost thou, as man, increase the stores of truth?
Then may thine own son afterwards excel thee.

FAUST

O happy he, who still renews
The hope, from Error's deeps to rise forever!
That which one does not know, one needs to use;
And what one knows, one uses never.
But let us not, by such despondence, so

The fortune of this hour embitter!
Mark how, beneath the evening sunlight's glow,
The green-embosomed houses glitter!
The glow retreats, done is the day of toil;
It yonder hastes, new fields of life exploring;
Ah, that no wing can lift me from the soil,
Upon its track to follow, follow soaring!
Then would I see eternal Evening gild
The silent world beneath me glowing,
On fire each mountain-peak, with peace each valley filled,
The silver brook to golden rivers flowing.
The mountain-chain, with all its gorges deep,
Would then no more impede my godlike motion;
And now before mine eyes expands the ocean
With all its bays, in shining sleep!
Yet, finally, the weary god is sinking;
The new-born impulse fires my mind,—
I hasten on, his beams eternal drinking,
The Day before me and the Night behind,
Above me heaven unfurled, the floor of waves beneath me,—
A glorious dream! though now the glories fade.
Alas! the wings that lift the mind no aid
Of wings to lift the body can bequeath me.
Yet in each soul is born the pleasure
Of yearning onward, upward and away,
When o'er our heads, lost in the vaulted azure,
The lark sends down his flickering lay,—
When over crags and piny highlands
The poising eagle slowly soars,
And over plains and lakes and islands
The crane sails by to other shores.
WAGNER
I've had, myself, at times, some odd caprices,
But never yet such impulse felt, as this is.
One soon fatigues, on woods and fields to look,
Nor would I beg the bird his wing to spare us:
How otherwise the mental raptures bear us
From page to page, from book to book!
Then winter nights take loveliness untold,
As warmer life in every limb had crowned you;
And when your hands unroll some parchment rare and old,
All Heaven descends, and opens bright around you!
FAUST
One impulse art thou conscious of, at best;

O, never seek to know the other!
Two souls, alas! reside within my breast,
And each withdraws from, and repels, its brother.
One with tenacious organs holds in love
And clinging lust the world in its embraces;
The other strongly sweeps, this dust above,
Into the high ancestral spaces.
If there be airy spirits near,
'Twixt Heaven and Earth on potent errands fleeing,
Let them drop down the golden atmosphere,
And bear me forth to new and varied being!
Yea, if a magic mantle once were mine,
To waft me o'er the world at pleasure,
I would not for the costliest stores of treasure—
Not for a monarch's robe—the gift resign.
WAGNER
Invoke not thus the well-known throng,
Which through the firmament diffused is faring,
And danger thousand-fold, our race to wrong.
In every quarter is preparing.
Swift from the North the spirit-fangs so sharp
Sweep down, and with their barbéd points assail you;
Then from the East they come, to dry and warp
Your lungs, till breath and being fail you:
If from the Desert sendeth them the South,
With fire on fire your throbbing forehead crowning,
The West leads on a host, to cure the drouth
Only when meadow, field, and you are drowning.
They gladly hearken, prompt for injury,—
Gladly obey, because they gladly cheat us;
From Heaven they represent themselves to be,
And lisp like angels, when with lies they meet us.
But, let us go! 'Tis gray and dusky all:
The air is cold, the vapors fall.
At night, one learns his house to prize:—
Why stand you thus, with such astonished eyes?
What, in the twilight, can your mind so trouble?
FAUST
Seest thou the black dog coursing there, through corn and
stubble?
WAGNER
Long since: yet deemed him not important in the least.
FAUST
Inspect him close: for what tak'st thou the beast?

41

WAGNER

Why, for a poodle who has lost his master,
And scents about, his track to find.

FAUST

Seest thou the spiral circles, narrowing faster,
Which he, approaching, round us seems to wind?
A streaming trail of fire, if I see rightly,
Follows his path of mystery.

WAGNER

It may be that your eyes deceive you slightly;
Naught but a plain black poodle do I see.

FAUST

It seems to me that with enchanted cunning
He snares our feet, some future chain to bind.

WAGNER

I see him timidly, in doubt, around us running,
Since, in his master's stead, two strangers doth he find.

FAUST

The circle narrows: he is near!

WAGNER

A dog thou seest, and not a phantom, here!
Behold him stop—upon his belly crawl—His
tail set wagging: canine habits, all!

FAUST

Come, follow us! Come here, at least!

WAGNER

'Tis the absurdest, drollest beast.
Stand still, and you will see him wait;
Address him, and he gambols straight;
If something's lost, he'll quickly bring it,—
Your cane, if in the stream you fling it.

FAUST

No doubt you're right: no trace of mind, I own,
Is in the beast: I see but drill, alone.

WAGNER

The dog, when he's well educated,
Is by the wisest tolerated.
Yes, he deserves your favor thoroughly,—
The clever scholar of the students, he!
(They pass in the city-gate.)

III
THE STUDY

FAUST
(Entering, with the poodle.)
Behind me, field and meadow sleeping,
I leave in deep, prophetic night,
Within whose dread and holy keeping
The better soul awakes to light.
The wild desires no longer win us,
The deeds of passion cease to chain;
The love of Man revives within us,
The love of God revives again.
Be still, thou poodle; make not such racket and riot!
Why at the threshold wilt snuffing be?
Behind the stove repose thee in quiet!
My softest cushion I give to thee.
As thou, up yonder, with running and leaping
Amused us hast, on the mountain's crest,
So now I take thee into my keeping,
A welcome, but also a silent, guest.
Ah, when, within our narrow chamber
The lamp with friendly lustre glows,
Flames in the breast each faded ember,
And in the heart, itself that knows.
Then Hope again lends sweet assistance,
And Reason then resumes her speech:
One yearns, the rivers of existence,
The very founts of Life, to reach.
Snarl not, poodle! To the sound that rises,
The sacred tones that my soul embrace,
This bestial noise is out of place.
We are used to see, that Man despises
What he never comprehends,
And the Good and the Beautiful vilipends,
Finding them often hard to measure:
Will the dog, like man, snarl his displeasure?
But ah! I feel, though will thereto be stronger,
Contentment flows from out my breast no longer.
Why must the stream so soon run dry and fail us,
And burning thirst again assail us?
Therein I've borne so much probation!
And yet, this want may be supplied us;

We call the Supernatural to guide us;
We pine and thirst for Revelation,
Which nowhere worthier is, more nobly sent,
Than here, in our New Testament.
I feel impelled, its meaning to determine,—
With honest purpose, once for all,
The hallowed Original
To change to my beloved German.
(He opens a volume, and commences.)
'Tis written: "In the Beginning was the Word."
Here am I balked: who, now can help afford?
The Word?—impossible so high to rate it;
And otherwise must I translate it.
If by the Spirit I am truly taught.
Then thus: "In the Beginning was the Thought"
This first line let me weigh completely,
Lest my impatient pen proceed too fleetly.
Is it the Thought which works, creates, indeed?
"In the Beginning was the Power," I read.
Yet, as I write, a warning is suggested,
That I the sense may not have fairly tested.
The Spirit aids me: now I see the light!
"In the Beginning was the Act," I write.
If I must share my chamber with thee,
Poodle, stop that howling, prithee!
Cease to bark and bellow!
Such a noisy, disturbing fellow
I'll no longer suffer near me.
One of us, dost hear me!
Must leave, I fear me.
No longer guest-right I bestow;
The door is open, art free to go.
But what do I see in the creature?
Is that in the course of nature?
Is't actual fact? or Fancy's shows?
How long and broad my poodle grows!
He rises mightily:
A canine form that cannot be!
What a spectre I've harbored thus!
He resembles a hippopotamus,
With fiery eyes, teeth terrible to see:
O, now am I sure of thee!
For all of thy half-hellish brood
The Key of Solomon is good.

SPIRITS (in the corridor)
Some one, within, is caught!
Stay without, follow him not!
Like the fox in a snare,
Quakes the old hell-lynx there.
Take heed—look about!
Back and forth hover,
Under and over,
And he'll work himself out.
If your aid avail him,
Let it not fail him;
For he, without measure,
Has wrought for our pleasure.
FAUST
First, to encounter the beast,
The Words of the Four be addressed:
Salamander, shine glorious!
Wave, Undine, as bidden!
Sylph, be thou hidden!
Gnome, be laborious!
Who knows not their sense
(These elements),—
Their properties
And power not sees,—
No mastery he inherits
Over the Spirits.
Vanish in flaming ether,
Salamander!
Flow foamingly together,
Undine!
Shine in meteor-sheen,
Sylph!
Bring help to hearth and shelf.
Incubus! Incubus!
Step forward, and finish thus!
Of the Four, no feature
Lurks in the creature.
Quiet he lies, and grins disdain:
Not yet, it seems, have I given him pain.
Now, to undisguise thee,
Hear me exorcise thee!
Art thou, my gay one,
Hell's fugitive stray-one?
The sign witness now,

45

Before which they bow,
The cohorts of Hell!
With hair all bristling, it begins to swell.
Base Being, hearest thou?
Knowest and fearest thou
The One, unoriginate,
Named inexpressibly,
Through all Heaven impermeate,
Pierced irredressibly!
Behind the stove still banned,
See it, an elephant, expand!
It fills the space entire,
Mist-like melting, ever faster.
'Tis enough: ascend no higher,—
Lay thyself at the feet of the Master!
Thou seest, not vain the threats I bring thee:
With holy fire I'll scorch and sting thee!
Wait not to know
The threefold dazzling glow!
Wait not to know
The strongest art within my hands!

MEPHISTOPHELES

(while the vapor is dissipating, steps forth from behind the
stove, in the costume of a Travelling Scholar.)
Why such a noise? What are my lord's commands?

FAUST

This was the poodle's real core,
A travelling scholar, then? The casus is diverting.

MEPHISTOPHELES

The learned gentleman I bow before:
You've made me roundly sweat, that's certain!

FAUST

What is thy name?

MEPHISTOPHELES

A question small, it seems,
For one whose mind the Word so much despises;
Who, scorning all external gleams,
The depths of being only prizes.

FAUST

With all you gentlemen, the name's a test,
Whereby the nature usually is expressed.
Clearly the latter it implies
In names like Beelzebub, Destroyer, Father of Lies.
Who art thou, then?

MEPHISTOPHELES
Part of that Power, not understood,
Which always wills the Bad, and always works the Good.
FAUST
What hidden sense in this enigma lies?
MEPHISTOPHELES
I am the Spirit that Denies!
And justly so: for all things, from the Void
Called forth, deserve to be destroyed:
'Twere better, then, were naught created.
Thus, all which you as Sin have rated,—
Destruction,—aught with Evil blent,—
That is my proper element.

FAUST
Thou nam'st thyself a part, yet show'st complete to me?
MEPHISTOPHELES
The modest truth I speak to thee.
If Man, that microcosmic fool, can see
Himself a whole so frequently,
Part of the Part am I, once All, in primal Night,—
Part of the Darkness which brought forth the Light,
The haughty Light, which now disputes the space,
And claims of Mother Night her ancient place.
And yet, the struggle fails; since Light, howe'er it weaves,
Still, fettered, unto bodies cleaves:
It flows from bodies, bodies beautifies;
By bodies is its course impeded;
And so, but little time is needed,
I hope, ere, as the bodies die, it dies!
FAUST
I see the plan thou art pursuing:
Thou canst not compass general ruin,
And hast on smaller scale begun.
MEPHISTOPHELES
And truly 'tis not much, when all is done.
That which to Naught is in resistance set,—
The Something of this clumsy world,—has yet,
With all that I have undertaken,
Not been by me disturbed or shaken:
From earthquake, tempest, wave, volcano's brand,
Back into quiet settle sea and land!
And that damned stuff, the bestial, human brood,—
What use, in having that to play with?
How many have I made away with!

And ever circulates a newer, fresher blood.
It makes me furious, such things beholding:
From Water, Earth, and Air unfolding,
A thousand germs break forth and grow,
In dry, and wet, and warm, and chilly;
And had I not the Flame reserved, why, really,
There's nothing special of my own to show!

FAUST

So, to the actively eternal
Creative force, in cold disdain
You now oppose the fist infernal,
Whose wicked clench is all in vain!
Some other labor seek thou rather,
Queer Son of Chaos, to begin!

MEPHISTOPHELES

Well, we'll consider: thou canst gather
My views, when next I venture in.
Might I, perhaps, depart at present?

FAUST

Why thou shouldst ask, I don't perceive.
Though our acquaintance is so recent,
For further visits thou hast leave.
The window's here, the door is yonder;
A chimney, also, you behold.

MEPHISTOPHELES

I must confess that forth I may not wander,
My steps by one slight obstacle controlled,—
The wizard's-foot, that on your threshold made is.

FAUST

The pentagram prohibits thee?
Why, tell me now, thou Son of Hades,
If that prevents, how cam'st thou in to me?
Could such a spirit be so cheated?

MEPHISTOPHELES

Inspect the thing: the drawing's not completed.
The outer angle, you may see,
Is open left—the lines don't fit it.

FAUST

Well,—Chance, this time, has fairly hit it!
And thus, thou'rt prisoner to me?
It seems the business has succeeded.

MEPHISTOPHELES

The poodle naught remarked, as after thee he speeded;
But other aspects now obtain:

The Devil can't get out again.

FAUST

Try, then, the open window-pane!

MEPHISTOPHELES

For Devils and for spectres this is law:
Where they have entered in, there also they withdraw.
The first is free to us; we're governed by the second.

FAUST

In Hell itself, then, laws are reckoned?
That's well! So might a compact be
Made with you gentlemen—and binding,—surely?

MEPHISTOPHELES

All that is promised shall delight thee purely;
No skinflint bargain shalt thou see.
But this is not of swift conclusion;
We'll talk about the matter soon.
And now, I do entreat this boon—
Leave to withdraw from my intrusion.

FAUST

One moment more I ask thee to remain,
Some pleasant news, at least, to tell me.

MEPHISTOPHELES

Release me, now! I soon shall come again;
Then thou, at will, mayst question and compel me.

FAUST

I have not snares around thee cast;
Thyself hast led thyself into the meshes.
Who traps the Devil, hold him fast!
Not soon a second time he'll catch a prey so precious.

MEPHISTOPHELES

An't please thee, also I'm content to stay,
And serve thee in a social station;
But stipulating, that I may
With arts of mine afford thee recreation.

FAUST

Thereto I willingly agree,
If the diversion pleasant be.

MEPHISTOPHELES

My friend, thou'lt win, past all pretences,
More in this hour to soothe thy senses,
Than in the year's monotony.
That which the dainty spirits sing thee,
The lovely pictures they shall bring thee,
Are more than magic's empty show.

Thy scent will be to bliss invited;
Thy palate then with taste delighted,
Thy nerves of touch ecstatic glow!
All unprepared, the charm I spin:
We're here together, so begin!
SPIRITS
Vanish, ye darking
Arches above him!
Loveliest weather,
Born of blue ether,
Break from the sky!
O that the darkling
Clouds had departed!
Starlight is sparkling,
Tranquiller-hearted
Suns are on high.
Heaven's own children
In beauty bewildering,
Waveringly bending,
Pass as they hover;
Longing unending
Follows them over.
They, with their glowing
Garments, out-flowing,
Cover, in going,
Landscape and bower,
Where, in seclusion,
Lovers are plighted,
Lost in illusion.
Bower on bower!
Tendrils unblighted!
Lo! in a shower
Grapes that o'ercluster
Gush into must, or
Flow into rivers
Of foaming and flashing
Wine, that is dashing
Gems, as it boundeth
Down the high places,
And spreading, surroundeth
With crystalline spaces,
In happy embraces,
Blossoming forelands,
Emerald shore-lands!

And the winged races
Drink, and fly onward—
Fly ever sunward
To the enticing
Islands, that flatter,
Dipping and rising
Light on the water!
Hark, the inspiring
Sound of their quiring!
See, the entrancing
Whirl of their dancing!
All in the air are
Freer and fairer.
Some of them scaling
Boldly the highlands,
Others are sailing,
Circling the islands;
Others are flying;
Life-ward all hieing,—
All for the distant
Star of existent
Rapture and Love!

MEPHISTOPHELES
He sleeps! Enough, ye fays! your airy number
Have sung him truly into slumber:
For this performance I your debtor prove.—
Not yet art thou the man, to catch the Fiend and hold him!—
With fairest images of dreams infold him,
Plunge him in seas of sweet untruth!
Yet, for the threshold's magic which controlled him,
The Devil needs a rat's quick tooth.
I use no lengthened invocation:
Here rustles one that soon will work my liberation.
The lord of rats and eke of mice,
Of flies and bed-bugs, frogs and lice,
Summons thee hither to the door-sill,
To gnaw it where, with just a morsel
Of oil, he paints the spot for thee:—
There com'st thou, hopping on to me!
To work, at once! The point which made me craven
Is forward, on the ledge, engraven.
Another bite makes free the door:
So, dream thy dreams, O Faust, until we meet once more!

FAUST (awaking)

Am I again so foully cheated?
Remains there naught of lofty spirit-sway,
But that a dream the Devil counterfeited,
And that a poodle ran away?

IV
THE STUDY
FAUST MEPHISTOPHELES

FAUST
A knock? Come in! Again my quiet broken?
MEPHISTOPHELES
'Tis I!
FAUST
Come in!
MEPHISTOPHELES
Thrice must the words be spoken.
FAUST
Come in, then!
MEPHISTOPHELES
Thus thou pleasest me.
I hope we'll suit each other well;
For now, thy vapors to dispel,
I come, a squire of high degree,
In scarlet coat, with golden trimming,
A cloak in silken lustre swimming,
A tall cock's-feather in my hat,
A long, sharp sword for show or quarrel,—
And I advise thee, brief and flat,
To don the self-same gay apparel,
That, from this den released, and free,
Life be at last revealed to thee!
FAUST
This life of earth, whatever my attire,
Would pain me in its wonted fashion.
Too old am I to play with passion;
Too young, to be without desire.
What from the world have I to gain?
Thou shalt abstain—renounce—refrain!
Such is the everlasting song
That in the ears of all men rings,—
That unrelieved, our whole life long,
Each hour, in passing, hoarsely sings.
In very terror I at morn awake,
Upon the verge of bitter weeping,
To see the day of disappointment break,
To no one hope of mine—not one—its promise keeping:—
That even each joy's presentiment
With wilful cavil would diminish,

53

With grinning masks of life prevent
My mind its fairest work to finish!
Then, too, when night descends, how anxiously
Upon my couch of sleep I lay me:
There, also, comes no rest to me,
But some wild dream is sent to fray me.
The God that in my breast is owned
Can deeply stir the inner sources;
The God, above my powers enthroned,
He cannot change external forces.
So, by the burden of my days oppressed,
Death is desired, and Life a thing unblest!

MEPHISTOPHELES

And yet is never Death a wholly welcome guest.

FAUST

O fortunate, for whom, when victory glances,
The bloody laurels on the brow he bindeth!
Whom, after rapid, maddening dances,
In clasping maiden-arms he findeth!
O would that I, before that spirit-power,
Ravished and rapt from life, had sunken!

MEPHISTOPHELES

And yet, by some one, in that nightly hour,
A certain liquid was not drunken.

FAUST

Eavesdropping, ha! thy pleasure seems to be.

MEPHISTOPHELES

Omniscient am I not; yet much is known to me.

FAUST

Though some familiar tone, retrieving
My thoughts from torment, led me on,
And sweet, clear echoes came, deceiving
A faith bequeathed from Childhood's dawn,
Yet now I curse whate'er entices
And snares the soul with visions vain;
With dazzling cheats and dear devices
Confines it in this cave of pain!
Cursed be, at once, the high ambition
Wherewith the mind itself deludes!
Cursed be the glare of apparition
That on the finer sense intrudes!
Cursed be the lying dream's impression
Of name, and fame, and laurelled brow!
Cursed, all that flatters as possession,

As wife and child, as knave and plow!
Cursed Mammon be, when he with treasures
To restless action spurs our fate!
Cursed when, for soft, indulgent leisures,
He lays for us the pillows straight!
Cursed be the vine's transcendent nectar,—
The highest favor Love lets fall!
Cursed, also, Hope!—cursed Faith, the spectre!
And cursed be Patience most of all!

CHORUS OF SPIRITS (invisible)

Woe! woe!
Thou hast it destroyed,
The beautiful world,
With powerful fist:
In ruin 'tis hurled,
By the blow of a demigod shattered!
The scattered
Fragments into the Void we carry,
Deploring
The beauty perished beyond restoring.
Mightier
For the children of men,
Brightlier
Build it again,
In thine own bosom build it anew!
Bid the new career
Commence,
With clearer sense,
And the new songs of cheer
Be sung thereto!

MEPHISTOPHELES

These are the small dependants
Who give me attendance.
Hear them, to deeds and passion
Counsel in shrewd old-fashion!
Into the world of strife,
Out of this lonely life
That of senses and sap has betrayed thee,
They would persuade thee.
This nursing of the pain forego thee,
That, like a vulture, feeds upon thy breast!
The worst society thou find'st will show thee
Thou art a man among the rest.
But 'tis not meant to thrust

Thee into the mob thou hatest!
I am not one of the greatest,
Yet, wilt thou to me entrust
Thy steps through life, I'll guide thee,—
Will willingly walk beside thee,—
Will serve thee at once and forever
With best endeavor,
And, if thou art satisfied,
Will as servant, slave, with thee abide.

FAUST

And what shall be my counter-service therefor?

MEPHISTOPHELES

The time is long: thou need'st not now insist.

FAUST

No—no! The Devil is an egotist,
And is not apt, without a why or wherefore,
"For God's sake," others to assist.
Speak thy conditions plain and clear!
With such a servant danger comes, I fear.

MEPHISTOPHELES

Here, an unwearied slave, I'll wear thy tether,
And to thine every nod obedient be:
When There again we come together,
Then shalt thou do the same for me.

FAUST

The There my scruples naught increases.
When thou hast dashed this world to pieces,
The other, then, its place may fill.
Here, on this earth, my pleasures have their sources;
Yon sun beholds my sorrows in his courses;
And when from these my life itself divorces,
Let happen all that can or will!
I'll hear no more: 'tis vain to ponder
If there we cherish love or hate,
Or, in the spheres we dream of yonder,
A High and Low our souls await.

MEPHISTOPHELES

In this sense, even, canst thou venture.
Come, bind thyself by prompt indenture,
And thou mine arts with joy shalt see:
What no man ever saw, I'll give to thee.

FAUST

Canst thou, poor Devil, give me whatsoever?
When was a human soul, in its supreme endeavor,

E'er understood by such as thou?
Yet, hast thou food which never satiates, now,—
The restless, ruddy gold hast thou,
That runs, quicksilver-like, one's fingers through,—
A game whose winnings no man ever knew,—
A maid that, even from my breast,
Beckons my neighbor with her wanton glances,
And Honor's godlike zest,
The meteor that a moment dances,—
Show me the fruits that, ere they're gathered, rot,
And trees that daily with new leafage clothe them!

MEPHISTOPHELES

Such a demand alarms me not:
Such treasures have I, and can show them.
But still the time may reach us, good my friend.
When peace we crave and more luxurious diet.

FAUST

When on an idler's bed I stretch myself in quiet.
There let, at once, my record end!
Canst thou with lying flattery rule me,
Until, self-pleased, myself I see,—
Canst thou with rich enjoyment fool me,
Let that day be the last for me!
The bet I offer.

MEPHISTOPHELES

Done!

FAUST

And heartily!
When thus I hail the Moment flying:
"Ah, still delay—thou art so fair!"
Then bind me in thy bonds undying,
My final ruin then declare!
Then let the death-bell chime the token.
Then art thou from thy service free!
The clock may stop, the hand be broken,
Then Time be finished unto me!

MEPHISTOPHELES

Consider well: my memory good is rated.

FAUST

Thou hast a perfect right thereto.
My powers I have not rashly estimated:
A slave am I, whate'er I do—
If thine, or whose? 'tis needless to debate it.

MEPHISTOPHELES

Then at the Doctors'-banquet I, to-day,
Will as a servant wait behind thee.
But one thing more! Beyond all risk to bind thee,
Give me a line or two, I pray.

FAUST

Demand'st thou, Pedant, too, a document?
Hast never known a man, nor proved his word's intent?
Is't not enough, that what I speak to-day
Shall stand, with all my future days agreeing?
In all its tides sweeps not the world away,
And shall a promise bind my being?
Yet this delusion in our hearts we bear:
Who would himself therefrom deliver?
Blest he, whose bosom Truth makes pure and fair!
No sacrifice shall he repent of ever.
Nathless a parchment, writ and stamped with care,
A spectre is, which all to shun endeavor.
The word, alas! dies even in the pen,
And wax and leather keep the lordship then.
What wilt from me, Base Spirit, say?—
Brass, marble, parchment, paper, clay?
The terms with graver, quill, or chisel, stated?
I freely leave the choice to thee.

MEPHISTOPHELES

Why heat thyself, thus instantly,
With eloquence exaggerated?
Each leaf for such a pact is good;
And to subscribe thy name thou'lt take a drop of blood.

FAUST

If thou therewith art fully satisfied,
So let us by the farce abide.

MEPHISTOPHELES

Blood is a juice of rarest quality.

FAUST

Fear not that I this pact shall seek to sever?
The promise that I make to thee
Is just the sum of my endeavor.
I have myself inflated all too high;
My proper place is thy estate:
The Mighty Spirit deigns me no reply,
And Nature shuts on me her gate.
The thread of Thought at last is broken,
And knowledge brings disgust unspoken.
Let us the sensual deeps explore,

To quench the fervors of glowing passion!
Let every marvel take form and fashion
Through the impervious veil it wore!
Plunge we in Time's tumultuous dance,
In the rush and roll of Circumstance!
Then may delight and distress,
And worry and success,
Alternately follow, as best they can:
Restless activity proves the man!

MEPHISTOPHELES

For you no bound, no term is set.
Whether you everywhere be trying,
Or snatch a rapid bliss in flying,
May it agree with you, what you get!
Only fall to, and show no timid balking.

FAUST

But thou hast heard, 'tis not of joy we're talking.
I take the wildering whirl, enjoyment's keenest pain,
Enamored hate, exhilarant disdain.
My bosom, of its thirst for knowledge sated,
Shall not, henceforth, from any pang be wrested,
And all of life for all mankind created
Shall be within mine inmost being tested:
The highest, lowest forms my soul shall borrow,
Shall heap upon itself their bliss and sorrow,
And thus, my own sole self to all their selves expanded,
I too, at last, shall with them all be stranded!

MEPHISTOPHELES

Believe me, who for many a thousand year
The same tough meat have chewed and tested,
That from the cradle to the bier
No man the ancient leaven has digested!
Trust one of us, this Whole supernal
Is made but for a God's delight!
He dwells in splendor single and eternal,
But us he thrusts in darkness, out of sight,
And you he dowers with Day and Night.

FAUST

Nay, but I will!

MEPHISTOPHELES

A good reply!
One only fear still needs repeating:
The art is long, the time is fleeting.
Then let thyself be taught, say I!

Go, league thyself with a poet,
Give the rein to his imagination,
Then wear the crown, and show it,
Of the qualities of his creation,—
The courage of the lion's breed,
The wild stag's speed,
The Italian's fiery blood,
The North's firm fortitude!
Let him find for thee the secret tether
That binds the Noble and Mean together.
And teach thy pulses of youth and pleasure
To love by rule, and hate by measure!
I'd like, myself, such a one to see:
Sir Microcosm his name should be.

FAUST

What am I, then, if 'tis denied my part
The crown of all humanity to win me,
Whereto yearns every sense within me?

MEPHISTOPHELES

Why, on the whole, thou'rt—what thou art.
Set wigs of million curls upon thy head, to raise thee,
Wear shoes an ell in height,—the truth betrays thee,
And thou remainest—what thou art.

FAUST

I feel, indeed, that I have made the treasure
Of human thought and knowledge mine, in vain;
And if I now sit down in restful leisure,
No fount of newer strength is in my brain:
I am no hair's-breadth more in height,
Nor nearer, to the Infinite,

MEPHISTOPHELES

Good Sir, you see the facts precisely
As they are seen by each and all.
We must arrange them now, more wisely,
Before the joys of life shall pall.
Why, Zounds! Both hands and feet are, truly—
And head and virile forces—thine:
Yet all that I indulge in newly,
Is't thence less wholly mine?
If I've six stallions in my stall,
Are not their forces also lent me?
I speed along, completest man of all,
As though my legs were four-and-twenty.
Take hold, then! let reflection rest,

And plunge into the world with zest!
I say to thee, a speculative wight
Is like a beast on moorlands lean,
That round and round some fiend misleads to evil plight,
While all about lie pastures fresh and green.

FAUST

Then how shall we begin?

MEPHISTOPHELES

We'll try a wider sphere.
What place of martyrdom is here!
Is't life, I ask, is't even prudence,
To bore thyself and bore the students?
Let Neighbor Paunch to that attend!
Why plague thyself with threshing straw forever?
The best thou learnest, in the end
Thou dar'st not tell the youngsters—never!
I hear one's footsteps, hither steering.

FAUST

To see him now I have no heart.

MEPHISTOPHELES

So long the poor boy waits a hearing,
He must not unconsoled depart.
Thy cap and mantle straightway lend me!
I'll play the comedy with art.
(He disguises himself.)
My wits, be certain, will befriend me.
But fifteen minutes' time is all I need;
For our fine trip, meanwhile, prepare thyself with speed!
[Exit FAUST.

MEPHISTOPHELES

(In FAUST'S long mantle.)
Reason and Knowledge only thou despise,
The highest strength in man that lies!
Let but the Lying Spirit bind thee
With magic works and shows that blind thee,
And I shall have thee fast and sure!—
Fate such a bold, untrammelled spirit gave him,
As forwards, onwards, ever must endure;
Whose over-hasty impulse drave him
Past earthly joys he might secure.
Dragged through the wildest life, will I enslave him,
Through flat and stale indifference;
With struggling, chilling, checking, so deprave him
That, to his hot, insatiate sense,

The dream of drink shall mock, but never lave him:
Refreshment shall his lips in vain implore—
Had he not made himself the Devil's, naught could save him,
Still were he lost forevermore!
(A STUDENT enters.)
STUDENT
A short time, only, am I here,
And come, devoted and sincere,
To greet and know the man of fame,
Whom men to me with reverence name.
MEPHISTOPHELES
Your courtesy doth flatter me:
You see a man, as others be.
Have you, perchance, elsewhere begun?
STUDENT
Receive me now, I pray, as one
Who comes to you with courage good,
Somewhat of cash, and healthy blood:
My mother was hardly willing to let me;
But knowledge worth having I fain would get me.
MEPHISTOPHELES
Then you have reached the right place now.
STUDENT
I'd like to leave it, I must avow;
I find these walls, these vaulted spaces
Are anything but pleasant places.
Tis all so cramped and close and mean;
One sees no tree, no glimpse of green,
And when the lecture-halls receive me,
Seeing, hearing, and thinking leave me.
MEPHISTOPHELES
All that depends on habitude.
So from its mother's breasts a child
At first, reluctant, takes its food,
But soon to seek them is beguiled.
Thus, at the breasts of Wisdom clinging,
Thou'lt find each day a greater rapture bringing.
STUDENT
I'll hang thereon with joy, and freely drain them;
But tell me, pray, the proper means to gain them.
MEPHISTOPHELES
Explain, before you further speak,
The special faculty you seek.
STUDENT

I crave the highest erudition;
And fain would make my acquisition
All that there is in Earth and Heaven,
In Nature and in Science too.
MEPHISTOPHELES
Here is the genuine path for you;
Yet strict attention must be given.
STUDENT
Body and soul thereon I'll wreak;
Yet, truly, I've some inclination
On summer holidays to seek
A little freedom and recreation.
MEPHISTOPHELES
Use well your time! It flies so swiftly from us;
But time through order may be won, I promise.
So, Friend (my views to briefly sum),
First, the collegium logicum.
There will your mind be drilled and braced,
As if in Spanish boots 'twere laced,
And thus, to graver paces brought,
'Twill plod along the path of thought,
Instead of shooting here and there,
A will-o'-the-wisp in murky air.
Days will be spent to bid you know,
What once you did at a single blow,
Like eating and drinking, free and strong,—
That one, two, three! thereto belong.
Truly the fabric of mental fleece
Resembles a weaver's masterpiece,
Where a thousand threads one treadle throws,
Where fly the shuttles hither and thither.
Unseen the threads are knit together.
And an infinite combination grows.
Then, the philosopher steps in
And shows, no otherwise it could have been:
The first was so, the second so,
Therefore the third and fourth are so;
Were not the first and second, then
The third and fourth had never been.
The scholars are everywhere believers,
But never succeed in being weavers.
He who would study organic existence,
First drives out the soul with rigid persistence;
Then the parts in his hand he may hold and class,

But the spiritual link is lost, alas!
Encheiresin natures, this Chemistry names,
Nor knows how herself she banters and blames!

STUDENT

I cannot understand you quite.

MEPHISTOPHELES

Your mind will shortly be set aright,
When you have learned, all things reducing,
To classify them for your using.

STUDENT

I feel as stupid, from all you've said,
As if a mill-wheel whirled in my head!

MEPHISTOPHELES

And after—first and foremost duty—Of
Metaphysics learn the use and beauty!
See that you most profoundly gain
What does not suit the human brain!
A splendid word to serve, you'll find
For what goes in—or won't go in—your mind.
But first, at least this half a year,
To order rigidly adhere;
Five hours a day, you understand,
And when the clock strikes, be on hand!
Prepare beforehand for your part
With paragraphs all got by heart,
So you can better watch, and look
That naught is said but what is in the book:
Yet in thy writing as unwearied be,
As did the Holy Ghost dictate to thee!

STUDENT

No need to tell me twice to do it!
I think, how useful 'tis to write;
For what one has, in black and white,
One carries home and then goes through it.

MEPHISTOPHELES

Yet choose thyself a faculty!

STUDENT

I cannot reconcile myself to Jurisprudence.

MEPHISTOPHELES

Nor can I therefore greatly blame you students:
I know what science this has come to be.
All rights and laws are still transmitted
Like an eternal sickness of the race,—
From generation unto generation fitted,

And shifted round from place to place.
Reason becomes a sham, Beneficence a worry:
Thou art a grandchild, therefore woe to thee!
The right born with us, ours in verity,
This to consider, there's, alas! no hurry.
STUDENT
My own disgust is strengthened by your speech:
O lucky he, whom you shall teach!
I've almost for Theology decided.
MEPHISTOPHELES
I should not wish to see you here misguided:
For, as regards this science, let me hint
'Tis very hard to shun the false direction;
There's so much secret poison lurking in 't,
So like the medicine, it baffles your detection.
Hear, therefore, one alone, for that is best, in sooth,
And simply take your master's words for truth.
On words let your attention centre!
Then through the safest gate you'll enter
The temple-halls of Certainty.
STUDENT
Yet in the word must some idea be.
MEPHISTOPHELES
Of course! But only shun too over-sharp a tension,
For just where fails the comprehension,
A word steps promptly in as deputy.
With words 'tis excellent disputing;
Systems to words 'tis easy suiting;
On words 'tis excellent believing;
No word can ever lose a jot from thieving.
STUDENT
Pardon! With many questions I detain you.
Yet must I trouble you again.
Of Medicine I still would fain
Hear one strong word that might explain you.
Three years is but a little space.
And, God! who can the field embrace?
If one some index could be shown,
'Twere easier groping forward, truly.
MEPHISTOPHELES (aside)
I'm tired enough of this dry tone,—
Must play the Devil again, and fully.
(Aloud)
To grasp the spirit of Medicine is easy:

65

Learn of the great and little world your fill,
To let it go at last, so please ye,
Just as God will!
In vain that through the realms of science you may drift;
Each one learns only—just what learn he can:
Yet he who grasps the Moment's gift,
He is the proper man.
Well-made you are, 'tis not to be denied,
The rest a bold address will win you;
If you but in yourself confide,
At once confide all others in you.
To lead the women, learn the special feeling!
Their everlasting aches and groans,
In thousand tones,
Have all one source, one mode of healing;
And if your acts are half discreet,
You'll always have them at your feet.
A title first must draw and interest them,
And show that yours all other arts exceeds;
Then, as a greeting, you are free to touch and test them,
While, thus to do, for years another pleads.
You press and count the pulse's dances,
And then, with burning sidelong glances,
You clasp the swelling hips, to see
If tightly laced her corsets be.
STUDENT
That's better, now! The How and Where, one sees.
MEPHISTOPHELES
My worthy friend, gray are all theories,
And green alone Life's golden tree.
STUDENT
I swear to you, 'tis like a dream to me.
Might I again presume, with trust unbounded,
To hear your wisdom thoroughly expounded?
MEPHISTOPHELES
Most willingly, to what extent I may.
STUDENT
I cannot really go away:
Allow me that my album first I reach you,—
Grant me this favor, I beseech you!
MEPHISTOPHELES
Assuredly.
(He writes, and returns the book.)
STUDENT (reads)

Eritis sicut Deus, scientes bonum et malum.
(Closes the book with reverence, and withdraws)
MEPHISTOPHELES
Follow the ancient text, and the snake thou wast ordered to trample!
With all thy likeness to God, thou'lt yet be a sorry example!
(FAUST enters.)
FAUST
Now, whither shall we go?
MEPHISTOPHELES
As best it pleases thee.
The little world, and then the great, we'll see.
With what delight, what profit winning,
Shalt thou sponge through the term beginning!
FAUST
Yet with the flowing beard I wear,
Both ease and grace will fail me there.
The attempt, indeed, were a futile strife;
I never could learn the ways of life.
I feel so small before others, and thence
Should always find embarrassments.
MEPHISTOPHELES
My friend, thou soon shalt lose all such misgiving:
Be thou but self-possessed, thou hast the art of living!
FAUST
How shall we leave the house, and start?
Where hast thou servant, coach and horses?
MEPHISTOPHELES
We'll spread this cloak with proper art,
Then through the air direct our courses.
But only, on so bold a flight,
Be sure to have thy luggage light.
A little burning air, which I shall soon prepare us,
Above the earth will nimbly bear us,
And, if we're light, we'll travel swift and clear:
I gratulate thee on thy new career!

FROSCH

I no one laughing? no one drinking?
I'll teach you how to grin, I'm thinking.
To-day you're like wet straw, so tame;
And usually you're all aflame.

BRANDER

Now that's your fault; from you we nothing see,
No beastliness and no stupidity.

FROSCH

(Pours a glass of wine over BRANDER'S head.)
There's both together!

BRANDER

Twice a swine!

FROSCH

You wanted them: I've given you mine.

SIEBEL

Turn out who quarrels—out the door!
With open throat sing chorus, drink and roar!
Up! holla! ho!

ALTMAYER

Woe's me, the fearful bellow!
Bring cotton, quick! He's split my ears, that fellow.

SIEBEL

When the vault echoes to the song,
One first perceives the bass is deep and strong.

FROSCH

Well said! and out with him that takes the least offence!
Ah, tara, lara da!

ALTMAYER

Ah, tara, lara, da!

FROSCH

The throats are tuned, commence!
(Sings.)
The dear old holy Roman realm,
How does it hold together?

BRANDER

A nasty song! Fie! a political song—
A most offensive song! Thank God, each morning, therefore,
That you have not the Roman realm to care for!
At least, I hold it so much gain for me,

That I nor Chancellor nor Kaiser be.
Yet also we must have a ruling head, I hope,
And so we'll choose ourselves a Pope.
You know the quality that can
Decide the choice, and elevate the man.
FROSCH
(sings)
Soar up, soar up, Dame Nightingale!
Ten thousand times my sweetheart hail!
SIEBEL
No, greet my sweetheart not! I tell you, I'll resent it.
FROSCH
My sweetheart greet and kiss! I dare you to prevent it!
(Sings.)
Draw the latch! the darkness makes:
Draw the latch! the lover wakes.
Shut the latch! the morning breaks
SIEBEL
Yes, sing away, sing on, and praise, and brag of her!
I'll wait my proper time for laughter:
Me by the nose she led, and now she'll lead you after.
Her paramour should be an ugly gnome,
Where four roads cross, in wanton play to meet her:
An old he-goat, from Blocksberg coming home,
Should his good-night in lustful gallop bleat her!
A fellow made of genuine flesh and blood
Is for the wench a deal too good.
Greet her? Not I: unless, when meeting,
To smash her windows be a greeting!
BRANDER (pounding on the table)
Attention! Hearken now to me!
Confess, Sirs, I know how to live.
Enamored persons here have we,
And I, as suits their quality,
Must something fresh for their advantage give.
Take heed! 'Tis of the latest cut, my strain,
And all strike in at each refrain!
(He sings.)
There was a rat in the cellar-nest,
Whom fat and butter made smoother:
He had a paunch beneath his vest
Like that of Doctor Luther.
The cook laid poison cunningly,
And then as sore oppressed was he

As if he had love in his bosom.
CHORUS (shouting)
As if he had love in his bosom!
BRANDER
He ran around, he ran about,
His thirst in puddles laving;
He gnawed and scratched the house throughout.
But nothing cured his raving.
He whirled and jumped, with torment mad,
And soon enough the poor beast had,
As if he had love in his bosom.
CHORUS
As if he had love in his bosom!
BRANDER
And driven at last, in open day,
He ran into the kitchen,
Fell on the hearth, and squirming lay,
In the last convulsion twitching.
Then laughed the murderess in her glee:
"Ha! ha! he's at his last gasp," said she,
"As if he had love in his bosom!"
CHORUS
As if he had love in his bosom!
SIEBEL
How the dull fools enjoy the matter!
To me it is a proper art
Poison for such poor rats to scatter.
BRANDER
Perhaps you'll warmly take their part?
ALTMAYER
The bald-pate pot-belly I have noted:
Misfortune tames him by degrees;
For in the rat by poison bloated
His own most natural form he sees.
FAUST AND MEPHISTOPHELES
MEPHISTOPHELES
Before all else, I bring thee hither
Where boon companions meet together,
To let thee see how smooth life runs away.
Here, for the folk, each day's a holiday:
With little wit, and ease to suit them,
They whirl in narrow, circling trails,
Like kittens playing with their tails?
And if no headache persecute them,

So long the host may credit give,
They merrily and careless live.
BRANDER
The fact is easy to unravel,
Their air's so odd, they've just returned from travel:
A single hour they've not been here.
FROSCH
You've verily hit the truth! Leipzig to me is dear:
Paris in miniature, how it refines its people!
SIEBEL
Who are the strangers, should you guess?
FROSCH
Let me alone! I'll set them first to drinking,
And then, as one a child's tooth draws, with cleverness,
I'll worm their secret out, I'm thinking.
They're of a noble house, that's very clear:
Haughty and discontented they appear.
BRANDER
They're mountebanks, upon a revel.
ALTMAYER
Perhaps.
FROSCH
Look out, I'll smoke them now!
MEPHISTOPHELES (to FAUST)
Not if he had them by the neck, I vow,
Would e'er these people scent the Devil!
FAUST Fair greeting, gentlemen!
SIEBEL
Our thanks: we give the same.
(Murmurs, inspecting MEPHISTOPHELES from the side.)
In one foot is the fellow lame?
MEPHISTOPHELES
Is it permitted that we share your leisure?
In place of cheering drink, which one seeks vainly here,
Your company shall give us pleasure.
ALTMAYER
A most fastidious person you appear.
FROSCH
No doubt 'twas late when you from Rippach started?
And supping there with Hans occasioned your delay?
MEPHISTOPHELES
We passed, without a call, to-day.
At our last interview, before we parted
Much of his cousins did he speak, entreating

71

That we should give to each his kindly greeting.
(He bows to FROSCH.)
ALTMAYER (aside)
You have it now! he understands.
SIEBEL
A knave sharp-set!
FROSCH
Just wait awhile: I'll have him yet.
MEPHISTOPHELES
If I am right, we heard the sound
Of well-trained voices, singing chorus;
And truly, song must here rebound
Superbly from the arches o'er us.
FROSCH
Are you, perhaps, a virtuoso?
MEPHISTOPHELES
O no! my wish is great, my power is only so-so.
ALTMAYER
Give us a song!
MEPHISTOPHELES
If you desire, a number.
SIEBEL
So that it be a bran-new strain!
MEPHISTOPHELES
We've just retraced our way from. Spain,
The lovely land of wine, and song, and slumber.
(Sings.)
There was a king once reigning,
Who had a big black flea—
FROSCH
Hear, hear! A flea! D'ye rightly take the jest?
I call a flea a tidy guest.
MEPHISTOPHELES (sings)
There was a king once reigning,
Who had a big black flea,
And loved him past explaining,
As his own son were he.
He called his man of stitches;
The tailor came straightway:
Here, measure the lad for breeches.
And measure his coat, I say!
BRANDER
But mind, allow the tailor no caprices:
Enjoin upon him, as his head is dear,

72

To most exactly measure, sew and shear,
So that the breeches have no creases!
MEPHISTOPHELES
In silk and velvet gleaming
He now was wholly drest—
Had a coat with ribbons streaming,
A cross upon his breast.
He had the first of stations,
A minister's star and name;
And also all his relations
Great lords at court became.
And the lords and ladies of honor
Were plagued, awake and in bed;
The queen she got them upon her,
The maids were bitten and bled.
And they did not dare to brush them,
Or scratch them, day or night:
We crack them and we crush them,
At once, whene'er they bite.
CHORUS (shouting)
We crack them and we crush them,
At once, whene'er they bite!
FROSCH Bravo! bravo! that was fine.
SIEBEL
Every flea may it so befall!
BRANDER
Point your fingers and nip them all!
ALTMAYER
Hurrah for Freedom! Hurrah for wine!
MEPHISTOPHELES
I fain would drink with you, my glass to Freedom clinking,
If 'twere a better wine that here I see you drinking.
SIEBEL
Don't let us hear that speech again!
MEPHISTOPHELES
Did I not fear the landlord might complain,
I'd treat these worthy guests, with pleasure,
To some from out our cellar's treasure.
SIEBEL
Just treat, and let the landlord me arraign!
FROSCH
And if the wine be good, our praises shall be ample.
But do not give too very small a sample;
For, if its quality I decide,

73

With a good mouthful I must be supplied.
ALTMAYER (aside)
They're from the Rhine! I guessed as much, before.
MEPHISTOPHELES
Bring me a gimlet here!
BRANDER
What shall therewith be done?
You've not the casks already at the door?
ALTMAYER
Yonder, within the landlord's box of tools, there's one!
MEPHISTOPHELES (takes the gimlet)
(To FROSCH.)
Now, give me of your taste some intimation.
FROSCH
How do you mean? Have you so many kinds?
MEPHISTOPHELES
The choice is free: make up your minds.
ALTMAYER (to FROSCH)
Aha! you lick your chops, from sheer anticipation.
FROSCH
Good! if I have the choice, so let the wine be Rhenish!
Our Fatherland can best the sparkling cup replenish.
MEPHISTOPHELES
(boring a hole in the edge of the table, at the place where
FROSCH sits)
Get me a little wax, to make the stoppers, quick!
ALTMAYER
Ah! I perceive a juggler's trick.
MEPHISTOPHELES (to BRANDER)
And you?
BRANDER
Champagne shall be my wine,
And let it sparkle fresh and fine!
MEPHISTOPHELES
(bores: in the meantime one has made the wax stoppers, and
plugged the holes with them.)
BRANDER
What's foreign one can't always keep quite clear of,
For good things, oft, are not so near;
A German can't endure the French to see or hear of,
Yet drinks their wines with hearty cheer.
SIEBEL
(as MEPHISTOPHELES approaches his seat)
For me, I grant, sour wine is out of place;

74

Fill up my glass with sweetest, will you?
MEPHISTOPHELES (boring)
Tokay shall flow at once, to fill you!
ALTMAYER
No—look me, Sirs, straight in the face!
I see you have your fun at our expense.
MEPHISTOPHELES
O no! with gentlemen of such pretence,
That were to venture far, indeed.
Speak out, and make your choice with speed! With what a vintage can I serve
you?
ALTMAYER
With any—only satisfy our need.
(After the holes have been bored and plugged)
MEPHISTOPHELES (with singular gestures)
Grapes the vine-stem bears,
Horns the he-goat wears!
The grapes are juicy, the vines are wood,
The wooden table gives wine as good!
Into the depths of Nature peer,—
Only believe there's a miracle here!
Now draw the stoppers, and drink your fill!
ALL
(as they draw out the stoppers, and the wine which has been
desired flows into the glass of each)
O beautiful fountain, that flows at will!
MEPHISTOPHELES
But have a care that you nothing spill!
(They drink repeatedly.)
ALL (sing)
As 'twere five hundred hogs, we feel
So cannibalic jolly!
MEPHISTOPHELES
See, now, the race is happy—it is free!
FAUST
To leave them is my inclination.
MEPHISTOPHELES
Take notice, first! their bestiality
Will make a brilliant demonstration.
SIEBEL
(drinks carelessly: the wine spills upon the earth, and turns to
flame)
Help! Fire! Help! Hell-fire is sent!
MEPHISTOPHELES (charming away the flame)

Be quiet, friendly element!
(To the revellers)
A bit of purgatory 'twas for this time, merely.
SIEBEL
What mean you? Wait!—you'll pay for't dearly!
You'll know us, to your detriment.
FROSCH
Don't try that game a second time upon us!
ALTMAYER
I think we'd better send him packing quietly.
SIEBEL
What, Sir! you dare to make so free,
And play your hocus-pocus on us!
MEPHISTOPHELES
Be still, old wine-tub.
SIEBEL
Broomstick, you!
You face it out, impertinent and heady?
BRANDER
Just wait! a shower of blows is ready.
ALTMAYER
(draws a stopper out of the table: fire flies in his face.)
I burn! I burn!
SIEBEL
'Tis magic! Strike—
The knave is outlawed! Cut him as you like!
(They draw their knives, and rush upon MEPHISTOPHELES.)
MEPHISTOPHELES (with solemn gestures)
False word and form of air,
Change place, and sense ensnare!
Be here—and there!
(They stand amazed and look at each other.)
ALTMAYER
Where am I? What a lovely land!
FROSCH
Vines? Can I trust my eyes?
SIEBEL
And purple grapes at hand!
BRANDER
Here, over this green arbor bending,
See what a vine! what grapes depending!
(He takes SIEBEL by the nose: the others do the same reciprocally,
and raise their knives.)
MEPHISTOPHELES (as above)

76

Loose, Error, from their eyes the band,
And how the Devil jests, be now enlightened!
(He disappears with FAUST: the revellers start and separate.)
SIEBEL
What happened?
ALTMAYER
How?
FROSCH
Was that your nose I tightened?
BRANDER (to SIEBEL)
And yours that still I have in hand?
ALTMAYER
It was a blow that went through every limb!
Give me a chair! I sink! my senses swim.
FROSCH
But what has happened, tell me now?
SIEBEL
Where is he? If I catch the scoundrel hiding,
He shall not leave alive, I vow.
ALTMAYER
I saw him with these eyes upon a wine-cask riding
Out of the cellar-door, just now.
Still in my feet the fright like lead is weighing.
(He turns towards the table.)
Why! If the fount of wine should still be playing?
SIEBEL
'Twas all deceit, and lying, false design!
FROSCH
And yet it seemed as I were drinking wine.
BRANDER
But with the grapes how was it, pray?
ALTMAYER
Shall one believe no miracles, just say!

VI

WITCHES' KITCHEN

(Upon a low hearth stands a great caldron, under which a fire
is burning. Various figures appear in the vapors which
rise from the caldron. An ape sits beside it, skims it, and
watches lest it boil over. The he-ape, with the young
ones, sits near and warms himself. Ceiling and walls are
covered with the most fantastic witch-implements.)
FAUST MEPHISTOPHELES
FAUST

These crazy signs of witches' craft repel me!
I shall recover, dost thou tell me,
Through this insane, chaotic play?
From an old hag shall I demand assistance?
And will her foul mess take away
Full thirty years from my existence?
Woe's me, canst thou naught better find!
Another baffled hope must be lamented:
Has Nature, then, and has a noble mind
Not any potent balsam yet invented?
MEPHISTOPHELES
Once more, my friend, thou talkest sensibly.
There is, to make thee young, a simpler mode and apter;
But in another book 'tis writ for thee,
And is a most eccentric chapter.
FAUST
Yet will I know it.
MEPHISTOPHELES
Good! the method is revealed
Without or gold or magic or physician.
Betake thyself to yonder field,
There hoe and dig, as thy condition;
Restrain thyself, thy sense and will
Within a narrow sphere to flourish;
With unmixed food thy body nourish;
Live with the ox as ox, and think it not a theft
That thou manur'st the acre which thou reapest;—
That, trust me, is the best mode left,
Whereby for eighty years thy youth thou keepest!
FAUST
I am not used to that; I cannot stoop to try it—
To take the spade in hand, and ply it.

The narrow being suits me not at all.
MEPHISTOPHELES
Then to thine aid the witch must call.
FAUST
Wherefore the hag, and her alone?
Canst thou thyself not brew the potion?
MEPHISTOPHELES
That were a charming sport, I own:
I'd build a thousand bridges meanwhile, I've a notion.
Not Art and Science serve, alone;
Patience must in the work be shown.
Long is the calm brain active in creation;
Time, only, strengthens the fine fermentation.
And all, belonging thereunto,
Is rare and strange, howe'er you take it:
The Devil taught the thing, 'tis true,
And yet the Devil cannot make it.
(Perceiving the Animals)
See, what a delicate race they be!
That is the maid! the man is he!
(To the Animals)
It seems the mistress has gone away?
THE ANIMALS
Carousing, to-day!
Off and about,
By the chimney out!
MEPHISTOPHELES
What time takes she for dissipating?
THE ANIMALS
While we to warm our paws are waiting.
MEPHISTOPHELES (to FAUST)
How findest thou the tender creatures?
FAUST
Absurder than I ever yet did see.
MEPHISTOPHELES
Why, just such talk as this, for me,
Is that which has the most attractive features!
(To the Animals)
But tell me now, ye cursed puppets,
Why do ye stir the porridge so?
THE ANIMALS
We're cooking watery soup for beggars.
MEPHISTOPHELES
Then a great public you can show.

THE HE-APE

(comes up and fawns on MEPHISTOPHELES)

O cast thou the dice!

Make me rich in a trice,

Let me win in good season!

Things are badly controlled,

And had I but gold,

So had I my reason.

MEPHISTOPHELES

How would the ape be sure his luck enhances.

Could he but try the lottery's chances!

(In the meantime the young apes have been playing with a
large ball, which they now roll forward.)

THE HE-APE

The world's the ball:

Doth rise and fall,

And roll incessant:

Like glass doth ring,

A hollow thing,—

How soon will't spring,

And drop, quiescent?

Here bright it gleams,

Here brighter seems:

I live at present!

Dear son, I say,

Keep thou away!

Thy doom is spoken!

'Tis made of clay,

And will be broken.

MEPHISTOPHELES

What means the sieve?

THE HE-APE (taking it down)

Wert thou the thief,

I'd know him and shame him.

(He runs to the SHE-APE, and lets her look through it.)

Look through the sieve!

Know'st thou the thief,

And darest not name him?

MEPHISTOPHELES (approaching the fire)

And what's this pot?

HE-APE AND SHE-APE

The fool knows it not!

He knows not the pot,

He knows not the kettle!

MEPHISTOPHELES

Impertinent beast!

THE HE-APE

Take the brush here, at least,
And sit down on the settle!

(He invites MEPHISTOPHELES to sit down.)

FAUST

(who during all this time has been standing before a mirror,
now approaching and now retreating from it)

What do I see? What heavenly form revealed
Shows through the glass from Magic's fair dominions!
O lend me, Love, the swiftest of thy pinions,
And bear me to her beauteous field!
Ah, if I leave this spot with fond designing,
If I attempt to venture near,
Dim, as through gathering mist, her charms appear!
A woman's form, in beauty shining!
Can woman, then, so lovely be?
And must I find her body, there reclining,
Of all the heavens the bright epitome?
Can Earth with such a thing be mated?

MEPHISTOPHELES

Why, surely, if a God first plagues Himself six days,
Then, self-contented, Bravo! says,
Must something clever be created.
This time, thine eyes be satiate!
I'll yet detect thy sweetheart and ensnare her,
And blest is he, who has the lucky fate,
Some day, as bridegroom, home to bear her.

(FAUST gazes continually in the mirror. MEPHISTOPHELES,
stretching himself out on the settle, and playing with the
brush, continues to speak.)

So sit I, like the King upon his throne:
I hold the sceptre, here,—and lack the crown alone.

THE ANIMALS

(who up to this time have been making all kinds of fantastic
movements together bring a crown to MEPHISTOPHELES
with great noise.)

O be thou so good
With sweat and with blood
The crown to belime!

(They handle the crown awkwardly and break it into two
pieces, with which they spring around.)

'Tis done, let it be!

We speak and we see,
We hear and we rhyme!
FAUST (before the mirror)
Woe's me! I fear to lose my wits.
MEPHISTOPHELES (pointing to the Animals)
My own head, now, is really nigh to sinking.
THE ANIMALS
If lucky our hits,
And everything fits,
'Tis thoughts, and we're thinking!
FAUST (as above)
My bosom burns with that sweet vision;
Let us, with speed, away from here!
MEPHISTOPHELES (in the same attitude)
One must, at least, make this admission—
They're poets, genuine and sincere.
(The caldron, which the SHE-APE has up to this time neglected
to watch, begins to boil over: there ensues a great flame,
which blazes out the chimney. The WITCH comes careering
down through the flame, with terrible cries.)
THE WITCH
Ow! ow! ow! ow!
The damnéd beast—the curséd sow!
To leave the kettle, and singe the Frau!
Accurséd fere!
(Perceiving FAUST and MEPHISTOPHELES.)
What is that here?
Who are you here?
What want you thus?
Who sneaks to us?
The fire-pain
Burn bone and brain!
(She plunges the skimming-ladle into the caldron, and scatters
flames towards FAUST, MEPHISTOPHELES, and the Animals.
The Animals whimper.)
MEPHISTOPHELES
(reversing the brush, which he has been holding in his hand,
and striding among the jars and glasses)
In two! in two!
There lies the brew!
There lies the glass!
The joke will pass,
As time, foul ass!
To the singing of thy crew.

(As the WITCH starts back, full of wrath and horror)
Ha! know'st thou me? Abomination, thou!
Know'st thou, at last, thy Lord and Master?
What hinders me from smiting now
Thee and thy monkey-sprites with fell disaster?
Hast for the scarlet coat no reverence?
Dost recognize no more the tall cock's-feather?
Have I concealed this countenance?—
Must tell my name, old face of leather?
THE WITCH
O pardon, Sir, the rough salute!
Yet I perceive no cloven foot;
And both your ravens, where are they now?
MEPHISTOPHELES
This time, I'll let thee 'scape the debt;
For since we two together met,
'Tis verily full many a day now.
Culture, which smooth the whole world licks,
Also unto the Devil sticks.
The days of that old Northern phantom now are over:
Where canst thou horns and tail and claws discover?
And, as regards the foot, which I can't spare, in truth,
'Twould only make the people shun me;
Therefore I've worn, like many a spindly youth,
False calves these many years upon me.
THE WITCH (dancing)
Reason and sense forsake my brain,
Since I behold Squire Satan here again!
MEPHISTOPHELES
Woman, from such a name refrain!
THE WITCH
Why so? What has it done to thee?
MEPHISTOPHELES
It's long been written in the Book of Fable;
Yet, therefore, no whit better men we see:
The Evil One has left, the evil ones are stable.
Sir Baron call me thou, then is the matter good;
A cavalier am I, like others in my bearing.
Thou hast no doubt about my noble blood:
See, here's the coat-of-arms that I am wearing!
(He makes an indecent gesture.)
THE WITCH (laughs immoderately)
Ha! ha! That's just your way, I know:
A rogue you are, and you were always so.

83

MEPHISTOPHELES (to FAUST)

My friend, take proper heed, I pray!

To manage witches, this is just the way.

THE WITCH

Wherein, Sirs, can I be of use?

MEPHISTOPHELES

Give us a goblet of the well-known juice!

But, I must beg you, of the oldest brewage;

The years a double strength produce.

THE WITCH

With all my heart! Now, here's a bottle,

Wherefrom, sometimes, I wet my throttle,

Which, also, not the slightest, stinks;

And willingly a glass I'll fill him.

(Whispering)

Yet, if this man without due preparation drinks,

As well thou know'st, within an hour 'twill kill him.

MEPHISTOPHELES

He is a friend of mine, with whom it will agree,

And he deserves thy kitchen's best potation:

Come, draw thy circle, speak thine adjuration,

And fill thy goblet full and free!

THE WITCH

(with fantastic gestures draws a circle and places mysterious
articles therein; meanwhile the glasses begin to ring, the
caldron to sound, and make a musical accompaniment.
Finally she brings a great book, and stations in the circle
the Apes, who are obliged to serve as reading-desk, and to
hold the torches. She then beckons FAUST to approach.)

FAUST (to MEPHISTOPHELES)

Now, what shall come of this? the creatures antic,

The crazy stuff, the gestures frantic,—

All the repulsive cheats I view,—

Are known to me, and hated, too.

MEPHISTOPHELES

O, nonsense! That's a thing for laughter;

Don't be so terribly severe!

She juggles you as doctor now, that, after,

The beverage may work the proper cheer.

(He persuades FAUST to step into the circle.)

THE WITCH

(begins to declaim, with much emphasis, from the book)

See, thus it's done!

Make ten of one,

And two let be,
Make even three,
And rich thou 'lt be.
Cast o'er the four!
From five and six
(The witch's tricks)
Make seven and eight,
'Tis finished straight!
And nine is one,
And ten is none.
This is the witch's once-one's-one!

FAUST

She talks like one who raves in fever.

MEPHISTOPHELES

Thou'lt hear much more before we leave her.
'Tis all the same: the book I can repeat,
Such time I've squandered o'er the history:
A contradiction thus complete
Is always for the wise, no less than fools, a mystery.
The art is old and new, for verily
All ages have been taught the matter,—
By Three and One, and One and Three,
Error instead of Truth to scatter.
They prate and teach, and no one interferes;
All from the fellowship of fools are shrinking.
Man usually believes, if only words he hears,
That also with them goes material for thinking!

THE WITCH (continues)

The lofty skill
Of Science, still
From all men deeply hidden!
Who takes no thought,
To him 'tis brought,
'Tis given unsought, unbidden!

FAUST

What nonsense she declaims before us!
My head is nigh to split, I fear:
It seems to me as if I hear
A hundred thousand fools in chorus.

MEPHISTOPHELES

O Sibyl excellent, enough of adjuration!
But hither bring us thy potation,
And quickly fill the beaker to the brim!
This drink will bring my friend no injuries:

85

He is a man of manifold degrees,
And many draughts are known to him.
(The WITCH, with many ceremonies, pours the drink into a
cup; as FAUST sets it to his lips, a light flame arises.)
Down with it quickly! Drain it off!
'Twill warm thy heart with new desire:
Art with the Devil hand and glove,
And wilt thou be afraid of fire?
(The WITCH breaks the circle: FAUST steps forth.)
MEPHISTOPHELES
And now, away! Thou dar'st not rest.
THE WITCH
And much good may the liquor do thee!
MEPHISTOPHELES (to the WITCH)
Thy wish be on Walpurgis Night expressed;
What boon I have, shall then be given unto thee.
THE WITCH
Here is a song, which, if you sometimes sing,
You'll find it of peculiar operation.
MEPHISTOPHELES (to FAUST)
Come, walk at once! A rapid occupation
Must start the needful perspiration,
And through thy frame the liquor's potence fling.
The noble indolence I'll teach thee then to treasure,
And soon thou'lt be aware, with keenest thrills of pleasure,
How Cupid stirs and leaps, on light and restless wing.
FAUST
One rapid glance within the mirror give me,
How beautiful that woman-form!
MEPHISTOPHELES
No, no! The paragon of all, believe me,
Thou soon shalt see, alive and warm.
(Aside)
Thou'lt find, this drink thy blood compelling,
Each woman beautiful as Helen!
 Street
 Street
VII
STREET
FAUST MARGARET (passing by)
FAUST
Fair lady, let it not offend you,
That arm and escort I would lend you!
MARGARET

I'm neither lady, neither fair,
And home I can go without your care.
[She releases herself, and exit.
FAUST
By Heaven, the girl is wondrous fair!
Of all I've seen, beyond compare;
So sweetly virtuous and pure,
And yet a little pert, be sure!
The lip so red, the cheek's clear dawn,
 So sweetly virtuous and pure, and yet a little pert be sure.
I'll not forget while the world rolls on!
How she cast down her timid eyes,
Deep in my heart imprinted lies:
How short and sharp of speech was she,
Why, 'twas a real ecstasy!
(MEPHISTOPHELES enters)
FAUST
Hear, of that girl I'd have possession!
MEPHISTOPHELES
Which, then?
FAUST
The one who just went by.
MEPHISTOPHELES
She, there? She's coming from confession,
Of every sin absolved; for I,
Behind her chair, was listening nigh.
So innocent is she, indeed,
That to confess she had no need.
I have no power o'er souls so green.
FAUST
And yet, she's older than fourteen.
MEPHISTOPHELES
How now! You're talking like Jack Rake,
Who every flower for himself would take,
And fancies there are no favors more,
Nor honors, save for him in store;
Yet always doesn't the thing succeed.
FAUST
Most Worthy Pedagogue, take heed!
Let not a word of moral law be spoken!
I claim, I tell thee, all my right;
And if that image of delight
Rest not within mine arms to-night,
At midnight is our compact broken.

MEPHISTOPHELES
But think, the chances of the case!
I need, at least, a fortnight's space,
To find an opportune occasion.
FAUST
Had I but seven hours for all,
I should not on the Devil call,
But win her by my own persuasion.
MEPHISTOPHELES
You almost like a Frenchman prate;
Yet, pray, don't take it as annoyance!
Why, all at once, exhaust the joyance?
Your bliss is by no means so great
As if you'd use, to get control,
All sorts of tender rigmarole,
And knead and shape her to your thought,
As in Italian tales 'tis taught.
FAUST
Without that, I have appetite.
MEPHISTOPHELES
But now, leave jesting out of sight!
I tell you, once for all, that speed
With this fair girl will not succeed;
By storm she cannot captured be;
We must make use of strategy.
FAUST
Get me something the angel keeps!
Lead me thither where she sleeps!
Get me a kerchief from her breast,—
A garter that her knee has pressed!
MEPHISTOPHELES
That you may see how much I'd fain
Further and satisfy your pain,
We will no longer lose a minute;
I'll find her room to-day, and take you in it.
FAUST
And shall I see—possess her?
MEPHISTOPHELES
No!
Unto a neighbor she must go,
And meanwhile thou, alone, mayst glow
With every hope of future pleasure,
Breathing her atmosphere in fullest measure.
FAUST

Can we go thither?
MEPHISTOPHELES
'Tis too early yet.
FAUST
A gift for her I bid thee get!
[Exit.
MEPHISTOPHELES
Presents at once? That's good: he's certain to get at her!
Full many a pleasant place I know,
And treasures, buried long ago:
I must, perforce, look up the matter. [Exit.

VIII

EVENING A SMALL, NEATLY KEPT CHAMBER

MARGARET
(plaiting and binding up the braids of her hair)
I'd something give, could I but say
Who was that gentleman, to-day.
Surely a gallant man was he,
And of a noble family;
And much could I in his face behold,—
And he wouldn't, else, have been so bold!
[Exit
MEPHISTOPHELES FAUST
MEPHISTOPHELES
Come in, but gently: follow me!
FAUST (after a moment's silence)
Leave me alone, I beg of thee!
MEPHISTOPHELES (prying about)
Not every girl keeps things so neat.
FAUST (looking around)
O welcome, twilight soft and sweet,
That breathes throughout this hallowed shrine!
Sweet pain of love, bind thou with fetters fleet
The heart that on the dew of hope must pine!
How all around a sense impresses
Of quiet, order, and content!
This poverty what bounty blesses!
What bliss within this narrow den is pent!
(He throws himself into a leathern arm-chair near the bed.)
Receive me, thou, that in thine open arms
Departed joy and pain wert wont to gather!
How oft the children, with their ruddy charms,
Hung here, around this throne, where sat the father!
Perchance my love, amid the childish band,
Grateful for gifts the Holy Christmas gave her,
Here meekly kissed the grandsire's withered hand.
I feel, O maid! thy very soul
Of order and content around me whisper,—
Which leads thee with its motherly control,
The cloth upon thy board bids smoothly thee unroll,
The sand beneath thy feet makes whiter, crisper.
O dearest hand, to thee 'tis given

To change this hut into a lower heaven!
And here!
(He lifts one of the bed-curtains.)
What sweetest thrill is in my blood!
Here could I spend whole hours, delaying:
Here Nature shaped, as if in sportive playing,
The angel blossom from the bud.
Here lay the child, with Life's warm essence
The tender bosom filled and fair,
And here was wrought, through holier, purer presence,
The form diviner beings wear!
And I? What drew me here with power?
How deeply am I moved, this hour!
What seek I? Why so full my heart, and sore?
Miserable Faust! I know thee now no more.
Is there a magic vapor here?
I came, with lust of instant pleasure,
And lie dissolved in dreams of love's sweet leisure!
Are we the sport of every changeful atmosphere?
And if, this moment, came she in to me,
How would I for the fault atonement render!
How small the giant lout would be,
Prone at her feet, relaxed and tender!
MEPHISTOPHELES
Be quick! I see her there, returning.
FAUST
Go! go! I never will retreat.
MEPHISTOPHELES
Here is a casket, not unmeet,
Which elsewhere I have just been earning.
Here, set it in the press, with haste!
I swear, 'twill turn her head, to spy it:
Some baubles I therein had placed,
That you might win another by it.
True, child is child, and play is play.
FAUST
I know not, should I do it?
MEPHISTOPHELES
Ask you, pray?
Yourself, perhaps, would keep the bubble?
Then I suggest, 'twere fair and just
To spare the lovely day your lust,
And spare to me the further trouble.
You are not miserly, I trust?

I rub my hands, in expectation tender—
(He places the casket in the press, and locks it again.)
Now quick, away!
The sweet young maiden to betray,
So that by wish and will you bend her;
And you look as though
To the lecture-hall you were forced to go,—
As if stood before you, gray and loath,
Physics and Metaphysics both!
But away!
[Exeunt.
MARGARET (with a lamp)
It is so close, so sultry, here!
(She opens the window)
And yet 'tis not so warm outside.
I feel, I know not why, such fear!—
Would mother came!—where can she bide?
My body's chill and shuddering,—
I'm but a silly, fearsome thing!
(She begins to sing while undressing)
There was a King in Thule,
Was faithful till the grave,—
To whom his mistress, dying,
A golden goblet gave.
Naught was to him more precious;
He drained it at every bout:
His eyes with tears ran over,
As oft as he drank thereout.
When came his time of dying,
The towns in his land he told,
Naught else to his heir denying
Except the goblet of gold.
He sat at the royal banquet
With his knights of high degree,
In the lofty hall of his fathers
In the Castle by the Sea.
There stood the old carouser,
And drank the last life-glow;
And hurled the hallowed goblet
Into the tide below.
He saw it plunging and filling,
And sinking deep in the sea:
Then fell his eyelids forever,
And never more drank he!

(She opens the press in order to arrange her clothes, and perceives
the casket of jewels.)
How comes that lovely casket here to me?
I locked the press, most certainly.
'Tis truly wonderful! What can within it be?
Perhaps 'twas brought by some one as a pawn,
And mother gave a loan thereon?
And here there hangs a key to fit:
I have a mind to open it.
What is that? God in Heaven! Whence came
Such things? Never beheld I aught so fair!
Rich ornaments, such as a noble dame
On highest holidays might wear!
How would the pearl-chain suit my hair?
Ah, who may all this splendor own?
(She adorns herself with the jewelry, and steps before the
mirror.)
Were but the ear-rings mine, alone!
One has at once another air.
What helps one's beauty, youthful blood?
One may possess them, well and good;
But none the more do others care.
They praise us half in pity, sure:
To gold still tends,
On gold depends
All, all! Alas, we poor!

IX

PROMENADE

(FAUST, walking thoughtfully up and down. To him MEPHISTOPHELES.)
MEPHISTOPHELES
By all love ever rejected! By hell-fire hot and unsparing!
I wish I knew something worse, that I might use it for
swearing!
FAUST
What ails thee? What is't gripes thee, elf?
A face like thine beheld I never.
MEPHISTOPHELES
I would myself unto the Devil deliver,
If I were not a Devil myself!
FAUST
Thy head is out of order, sadly:
It much becomes thee to be raving madly.
MEPHISTOPHELES
Just think, the pocket of a priest should get
The trinkets left for Margaret!
The mother saw them, and, instanter,
A secret dread began to haunt her.
Keen scent has she for tainted air;
She snuffs within her book of prayer,
And smells each article, to see
If sacred or profane it be;
So here she guessed, from every gem,
That not much blessing came with them.
"My child," she said, "ill-gotten good
Ensnares the soul, consumes the blood.
Before the Mother of God we'll lay it;
With heavenly manna she'll repay it!"
But Margaret thought, with sour grimace,
"A gift-horse is not out of place,
And, truly! godless cannot be
The one who brought such things to me."
A parson came, by the mother bidden:
He saw, at once, where the game was hidden,
And viewed it with a favor stealthy.
He spake: "That is the proper view,—
Who overcometh, winneth too.
The Holy Church has a stomach healthy:
Hath eaten many a land as forfeit,

94

And never yet complained of surfeit:
The Church alone, beyond all question,
Has for ill-gotten goods the right digestion."
FAUST
A general practice is the same,
Which Jew and King may also claim.
MEPHISTOPHELES
Then bagged the spangles, chains, and rings,
As if but toadstools were the things,
And thanked no less, and thanked no more
Than if a sack of nuts he bore,—
Promised them fullest heavenly pay,
And deeply edified were they.
FAUST
And Margaret?
MEPHISTOPHELES
Sits unrestful still,
And knows not what she should, or will;
Thinks on the jewels, day and night,
But more on him who gave her such delight.
FAUST
The darling's sorrow gives me pain.
Get thou a set for her again!
The first was not a great display.
MEPHISTOPHELES
O yes, the gentleman finds it all child's-play!
FAUST
Fix and arrange it to my will;
And on her neighbor try thy skill!
Don't be a Devil stiff as paste,
But get fresh jewels to her taste!
MEPHISTOPHELES
Yes, gracious Sir, in all obedience!
[Exit FAUST.
Such an enamored fool in air would blow
Sun, moon, and all the starry legions,
To give his sweetheart a diverting show.
[Exit.

MARTHA (solus)
God forgive my husband, yet he
Hasn't done his duty by me!
Off in the world he went straightway,—
Left me lie in the straw where I lay.
And, truly, I did naught to fret him:
God knows I loved, and can't forget him!
(She weeps.)
Perhaps he's even dead! Ah, woe!—
Had I a certificate to show!
MARGARET (comes)
Dame Martha!
MARTHA
Margaret! what's happened thee?
MARGARET
I scarce can stand, my knees are trembling!
I find a box, the first resembling,
Within my press! Of ebony,—
And things, all splendid to behold,
And richer far than were the old.
MARTHA
You mustn't tell it to your mother!
'Twould go to the priest, as did the other.
MARGARET
Ah, look and see—just look and see!
MARTHA (adorning her)
O, what a blessed luck for thee!
MARGARET
But, ah! in the streets I dare not bear them,
Nor in the church be seen to wear them.
MARTHA
Yet thou canst often this way wander,
And secretly the jewels don,
Walk up and down an hour, before the mirror yonder,—
We'll have our private joy thereon.
And then a chance will come, a holiday,
When, piece by piece, can one the things abroad display,
A chain at first, then other ornament:
Thy mother will not see, and stories we'll invent.
MARGARET

Whoever could have brought me things so precious?
That something's wrong, I feel suspicious.
(A knock)
Good Heaven! My mother can that have been?
MARTHA (peeping through the blind)
'Tis some strange gentleman.—Come in!
(MEPHISTOPHELES enters.)
MEPHISTOPHELES
That I so boldly introduce me,
I beg you, ladies, to excuse me.
(Steps back reverently, on seeing MARGARET.)
For Martha Schwerdtlein I'd inquire!
MARTHA
I'm she: what does the gentleman desire?
MEPHISTOPHELES (aside to her)
It is enough that you are she:
You've a visitor of high degree.
Pardon the freedom I have ta'en,—
Will after noon return again.
MARTHA (aloud)
Of all things in the world! Just hear—
He takes thee for a lady, dear!
MARGARET
I am a creature young and poor:
The gentleman's too kind, I'm sure.
The jewels don't belong to me.
MEPHISTOPHELES
Ah, not alone the jewelry!
The look, the manner, both betray—
Rejoiced am I that I may stay!
MARTHA
What is your business? I would fain—
MEPHISTOPHELES
I would I had a more cheerful strain!
Take not unkindly its repeating:
Your husband's dead, and sends a greeting.
MARTHA
Is dead? Alas, that heart so true!
My husband dead! Let me die, too!
MARGARET
Ah, dearest dame, let not your courage fail!
MEPHISTOPHELES
Hear me relate the mournful tale!
MARGARET

97

Therefore I'd never love, believe me!
A loss like this to death would grieve me.
MEPHISTOPHELES
Joy follows woe, woe after joy comes flying.
MARTHA
Relate his life's sad close to me!
MEPHISTOPHELES
In Padua buried, he is lying
Beside the good Saint Antony,
Within a grave well consecrated,
For cool, eternal rest created.
MARTHA
He gave you, further, no commission?
MEPHISTOPHELES
Yes, one of weight, with many sighs:
Three hundred masses buy, to save him from perdition!
My hands are empty, otherwise.
MARTHA
What! Not a pocket-piece? no jewelry?
What every journeyman within his wallet spares,
And as a token with him bears,
And rather starves or begs, than loses?
MEPHISTOPHELES
Madam, it is a grief to me;
Yet, on my word, his cash was put to proper uses.
Besides, his penitence was very sore,
And he lamented his ill fortune all the more.
MARGARET
Alack, that men are so unfortunate!
Surely for his soul's sake full many a prayer I'll proffer.
MEPHISTOPHELES
You well deserve a speedy marriage-offer:
You are so kind, compassionate.
MARGARET
O, no! As yet, it would not do.
MEPHISTOPHELES
If not a husband, then a beau for you!
It is the greatest heavenly blessing,
To have a dear thing for one's caressing.
MARGARET
The country's custom is not so.
MEPHISTOPHELES
Custom, or not! It happens, though.
MARTHA

Continue, pray!
MEPHISTOPHELES
I stood beside his bed of dying.
'Twas something better than manure,—
Half-rotten straw: and yet, he died a Christian, sure,
And found that heavier scores to his account were lying.
He cried: "I find my conduct wholly hateful!
To leave my wife, my trade, in manner so ungrateful!
Ah, the remembrance makes me die!
Would of my wrong to her I might be shriven!"
MARTHA (weeping)
The dear, good man! Long since was he forgiven.
MEPHISTOPHELES
"Yet she, God knows! was more to blame than I."
MARTHA
He lied! What! On the brink of death he slandered?
MEPHISTOPHELES
In the last throes his senses wandered,
If I such things but half can judge.
He said: "I had no time for play, for gaping freedom:
First children, and then work for bread to feed 'em,—
For bread, in the widest sense, to drudge,
And could not even eat my share in peace and quiet!"
MARTHA
Had he all love, all faith forgotten in his riot?
My work and worry, day and night?
MEPHISTOPHELES
Not so: the memory of it touched him quite.
Said he: "When I from Malta went away
My prayers for wife and little ones were zealous,
And such a luck from Heaven befell us,
We made a Turkish merchantman our prey,
That to the Soldan bore a mighty treasure.
Then I received, as was most fit,
Since bravery was paid in fullest measure,
My well-apportioned share of it."
MARTHA
Say, how? Say, where? If buried, did he own it?
MEPHISTOPHELES
Who knows, now, whither the four winds have blown it?
A fair young damsel took him in her care,
As he in Naples wandered round, unfriended;
And she much love, much faith to him did bear,
So that he felt it till his days were ended.

MARTHA

The villain! From his children thieving!
Even all the misery on him cast
Could not prevent his shameful way of living!

MEPHISTOPHELES

But see! He's dead therefrom, at last.
Were I in your place, do not doubt me,
I'd mourn him decently a year,
And for another keep, meanwhile, my eyes about me.

MARTHA

Ah, God! another one so dear
As was my first, this world will hardly give me.
There never was a sweeter fool than mine,
Only he loved to roam and leave me,
And foreign wenches and foreign wine,
And the damned throw of dice, indeed.

MEPHISTOPHELES

Well, well! That might have done, however,
If he had only been as clever,
And treated your slips with as little heed.
I swear, with this condition, too,
I would, myself, change rings with you.

MARTHA

The gentleman is pleased to jest.

MEPHISTOPHELES

I'll cut away, betimes, from here:
She'd take the Devil at his word, I fear.
(To MARGARET)
How fares the heart within your breast?

MARGARET

What means the gentleman?

MEPHISTOPHELES (aside)

Sweet innocent, thou art!
(Aloud.)
Ladies, farewell!

MARGARET

Farewell!

MARTHA

A moment, ere we part!
I'd like to have a legal witness,
Where, how, and when he died, to certify his fitness.
Irregular ways I've always hated;
I want his death in the weekly paper stated.

MEPHISTOPHELES

Yes, my good dame, a pair of witnesses
Always the truth establishes.
I have a friend of high condition,
Who'll also add his deposition.
I'll bring him here.

MARTHA

Good Sir, pray do!

MEPHISTOPHELES

And this young lady will be present, too?
A gallant youth! has travelled far:
Ladies with him delighted are.

MARGARET

Before him I should blush, ashamed.

MEPHISTOPHELES

Before no king that could be named!

MARTHA

Behind the house, in my garden, then,
This eve we'll expect the gentlemen.

XI

A STREET
FAUST MEPHISTOPHELES

FAUST
How is it? under way? and soon complete?
MEPHISTOPHELES
Ah, bravo! Do I find you burning?
Well, Margaret soon will still your yearning:
At Neighbor Martha's you'll this evening meet.
A fitter woman ne'er was made
To ply the pimp and gypsy trade!
FAUST
Tis well.
MEPHISTOPHELES
Yet something is required from us.
FAUST
One service pays the other thus.
MEPHISTOPHELES
We've but to make a deposition valid
That now her husband's limbs, outstretched and pallid,
At Padua rest, in consecrated soil.
FAUST
Most wise! And first, of course, we'll make the journey
thither?
MEPHISTOPHELES
Sancta simplicitas! no need of such a toil;
Depose, with knowledge or without it, either!
FAUST
If you've naught better, then, I'll tear your pretty plan!
MEPHISTOPHELES
Now, there you are! O holy man!
Is it the first time in your life you're driven
To bear false witness in a case?
Of God, the world and all that in it has a place,
Of Man, and all that moves the being of his race,
Have you not terms and definitions given
With brazen forehead, daring breast?
And, if you'll probe the thing profoundly,
Knew you so much—and you'll confess it roundly!—
As here of Schwerdtlein's death and place of rest?
FAUST
Thou art, and thou remain'st, a sophist, liar.

MEPHISTOPHELES
Yes, knew I not more deeply thy desire.
For wilt thou not, no lover fairer,
Poor Margaret flatter, and ensnare her,
And all thy soul's devotion swear her?
FAUST
And from my heart.
MEPHISTOPHELES
'Tis very fine!
Thine endless love, thy faith assuring,
The one almighty force enduring,—
Will that, too, prompt this heart of thine?
FAUST
Hold! hold! It will!—If such my flame,
And for the sense and power intense
I seek, and cannot find, a name;
Then range with all my senses through creation,
Craving the speech of inspiration,
And call this ardor, so supernal,
Endless, eternal and eternal,—
Is that a devilish lying game?
MEPHISTOPHELES
And yet I'm right!
FAUST
Mark this, I beg of thee!
And spare my lungs henceforth: whoever
Intends to have the right, if but his
tongue be clever,
Will have it, certainly.
But come: the further talking brings
disgust,
For thou art right, especially since I
must.

XII
GARDEN

(MARGARET on FAUST'S arm. MARTHA and MEPHISTOPHELES walking up and down.)

MARGARET

I feel, the gentleman allows for me,
Demeans himself, and shames me by it;
A traveller is so used to be
Kindly content with any diet.
I know too well that my poor gossip can
Ne'er entertain such an experienced man.

FAUST

A look from thee, a word, more entertains
Than all the lore of wisest brains.

(He kisses her hand.)

MARGARET

Don't incommode yourself! How could you ever kiss it!
It is so ugly, rough to see!
What work I do,—how hard and steady is it!
Mother is much too close with me.

[They pass.

MARTHA

And you, Sir, travel always, do you not?

MEPHISTOPHELES

Alas, that trade and duty us so harry!
With what a pang one leaves so many a spot,
And dares not even now and then to tarry!

MARTHA

In young, wild years it suits your ways,
This round and round the world in freedom sweeping;
But then come on the evil days,
And so, as bachelor, into his grave a-creeping,
None ever found a thing to praise.

MEPHISTOPHELES

I dread to see how such a fate advances.

MARTHA

Then, worthy Sir, improve betimes your chances!

[They pass.

MARGARET

Yes, out of sight is out of mind!
Your courtesy an easy grace is;
But you have friends in other places,

And sensibler than I, you'll find.
FAUST
Trust me, dear heart! what men call sensible
Is oft mere vanity and narrowness.
MARGARET
How so?
FAUST
Ah, that simplicity and innocence ne'er know
Themselves, their holy value, and their spell!
That meekness, lowliness, the highest graces
Which Nature portions out so lovingly—
MARGARET
So you but think a moment's space on me,
All times I'll have to think on you, all places!
FAUST
No doubt you're much alone?
MARGARET
Yes, for our household small has grown,
Yet must be cared for, you will own.
We have no maid: I do the knitting, sewing, sweeping,
The cooking, early work and late, in fact;
And mother, in her notions of housekeeping,
Is so exact!
Not that she needs so much to keep expenses down:
We, more than others, might take comfort, rather:
A nice estate was left us by my father,
A house, a little garden near the town.
But now my days have less of noise and hurry;
My brother is a soldier,
My little sister's dead.
True, with the child a troubled life I led,
Yet I would take again, and willing, all the worry,
So very dear was she.
FAUST
An angel, if like thee!
MARGARET
I brought it up, and it was fond of me.
Father had died before it saw the light,
And mother's case seemed hopeless quite,
So weak and miserable she lay;
And she recovered, then, so slowly, day by day.
She could not think, herself, of giving
The poor wee thing its natural living;
And so I nursed it all alone

With milk and water: 'twas my own.
Lulled in my lap with many a song,
It smiled, and tumbled, and grew strong.

FAUST

The purest bliss was surely then thy dower.

MARGARET

But surely, also, many a weary hour.
I kept the baby's cradle near
My bed at night: if 't even stirred, I'd guess it,
And waking, hear.
And I must nurse it, warm beside me press it,
And oft, to quiet it, my bed forsake,
And dandling back and forth the restless creature take,
Then at the wash-tub stand, at morning's break;
And then the marketing and kitchen-tending,
Day after day, the same thing, never-ending.
One's spirits, Sir, are thus not always good,
But then one learns to relish rest and food.

[They pass.

MARTHA

Yes, the poor women are bad off, 'tis true:
A stubborn bachelor there's no converting.

MEPHISTOPHELES

It but depends upon the like of you,
And I should turn to better ways than flirting.

MARTHA

Speak plainly, Sir, have you no one detected?
Has not your heart been anywhere subjected?

MEPHISTOPHELES

The proverb says: One's own warm hearth
And a good wife, are gold and jewels worth.

MARTHA

I mean, have you not felt desire, though ne'er so slightly?

MEPHISTOPHELES

I've everywhere, in fact, been entertained politely.

MARTHA

I meant to say, were you not touched in earnest, ever?

MEPHISTOPHELES

One should allow one's self to jest with ladies never.

MARTHA Ah, you don't understand!

MEPHISTOPHELES

I'm sorry I'm so blind: But I am sure—that you are very kind.

[They pass.

FAUST

And me, thou angel! didst thou recognize,
As through the garden-gate I came?

MARGARET

Did you not see it? I cast down my eyes.

FAUST

And thou forgiv'st my freedom, and the blame
To my impertinence befitting,
As the Cathedral thou wert quitting?

MARGARET

I was confused, the like ne'er happened me;
No one could ever speak to my discredit.
Ah, thought I, in my conduct has he read it—
Something immodest or unseemly free?
He seemed to have the sudden feeling
That with this wench 'twere very easy dealing.
I will confess, I knew not what appeal
On your behalf, here, in my bosom grew;
But I was angry with myself, to feel
That I could not be angrier with you.

FAUST

Sweet darling!

MARGARET

Wait a while!

(She plucks a star-flower, and pulls off the leaves, one after
the other.)

FAUST

Shall that a nosegay be?

MARGARET

No, it is just in play.

FAUST

How?

MARGARET

Go! you'll laugh at me.

(She pulls off the leaves and murmurs.)

FAUST

What murmurest thou?

MARGARET (half aloud)

He loves me—loves me not.

FAUST

Thou sweet, angelic soul!

MARGARET (continues)

Loves me—not—loves me—not—
(plucking the last leaf, she cries with frank delight;)
He loves me!

FAUST

Yes, child! and let this blossom-word
For thee be speech divine! He loves thee!
Ah, know'st thou what it means? He loves thee!
(He grasps both her hands.)

MARGARET

I'm all a-tremble!

FAUST

O tremble not! but let this look,
Let this warm clasp of hands declare thee
What is unspeakable!
To yield one wholly, and to feel a rapture
In yielding, that must be eternal!
Eternal!—for the end would be despair.
No, no,—no ending! no ending!

MARTHA (coming forward)

The night is falling.

MEPHISTOPHELES

Ay! we must away.

MARTHA

I'd ask you, longer here to tarry,
But evil tongues in this town have full play.
It's as if nobody had nothing to fetch and carry,
Nor other labor,
But spying all the doings of one's neighbor:
And one becomes the talk, do whatsoe'er one may.
Where is our couple now?

MEPHISTOPHELES

Flown up the alley yonder,
The wilful summer-birds!

MARTHA

He seems of her still fonder.

MEPHISTOPHELES

And she of him. So runs the world away!

XIII
A GARDEN-ARBOR

(MARGARET comes in, conceals herself behind the door, puts her finger to her lips, and peeps through the crack.)

MARGARET
He comes!
FAUST (entering)
Ah, rogue! a tease thou art:
I have thee! (He kisses her.)
MARGARET
(clasping him, and returning the kiss)
Dearest man! I love thee from my heart.
(MEPHISTOPHELES knocks)
FAUST (stamping his foot)
Who's there?
MEPHISTOPHELES
A friend!
FAUST
A beast!
MEPHISTOPHELES
Tis time to separate.
MARTHA (coming)
Yes, Sir, 'tis late.
FAUST
May I not, then, upon you wait?
MARGARET
My mother would—farewell!
FAUST
Ah, can I not remain?
Farewell!
MARTHA
Adieu!
MARGARET
And soon to meet again!
[Exeunt FAUST and MEPHISTOPHELES.
MARGARET
Dear God! However is it, such
A man can think and know so much?
I stand ashamed and in amaze,
And answer "Yes" to all he says,
A poor, unknowing child! and he—
I can't think what he finds in me!   [Exit.

XIV
FOREST AND CAVERN

FAUST (solus)
Spirit sublime, thou gav'st me, gav'st me all
For which I prayed. Not unto me in vain
Hast thou thy countenance revealed in fire.
Thou gav'st me Nature as a kingdom grand,
With power to feel and to enjoy it. Thou
Not only cold, amazed acquaintance yield'st,
But grantest, that in her profoundest breast
I gaze, as in the bosom of a friend.
The ranks of living creatures thou dost lead
Before me, teaching me to know my brothers
In air and water and the silent wood.
And when the storm in forests roars and grinds,
The giant firs, in falling, neighbor boughs
And neighbor trunks with crushing weight bear down,
And falling, fill the hills with hollow thunders,—
Then to the cave secure thou leadest me,
Then show'st me mine own self, and in my breast
The deep, mysterious miracles unfold.
And when the perfect moon before my gaze
Comes up with soothing light, around me float
From every precipice and thicket damp
The silvery phantoms of the ages past,
And temper the austere delight of thought.
That nothing can be perfect unto Man
I now am conscious. With this ecstasy,
Which brings me near and nearer to the Gods,
Thou gav'st the comrade, whom I now no more
Can do without, though, cold and scornful, he
Demeans me to myself, and with a breath,
A word, transforms thy gifts to nothingness.
Within my breast he fans a lawless fire,
Unwearied, for that fair and lovely form:
Thus in desire I hasten to enjoyment,
And in enjoyment pine to feel desire.
(MEPHISTOPHELES enters.)
MEPHISTOPHELES
Have you not led this life quite long enough?
How can a further test delight you?
'Tis very well, that once one tries the stuff,

110

But something new must then requite you.
FAUST
Would there were other work for thee!
To plague my day auspicious thou returnest.
MEPHISTOPHELES
Well! I'll engage to let thee be:
Thou darest not tell me so in earnest.
The loss of thee were truly very slight,—
comrade crazy, rude, repelling:
 Faust
One has one's hands full all the day and night;
If what one does, or leaves undone, is right,
From such a face as thine there is no telling.
FAUST

There is, again, thy proper tone!—
That thou hast bored me, I must thankful be!
MEPHISTOPHELES
Poor Son of Earth, how couldst thou thus alone
Have led thy life, bereft of me?
I, for a time, at least, have worked thy cure;
Thy fancy's rickets plague thee not at all:
Had I not been, so hadst thou, sure,
Walked thyself off this earthly ball
Why here to caverns, rocky hollows slinking,
Sit'st thou, as 'twere an owl a-blinking?
Why suck'st, from sodden moss and dripping stone,
Toad like, thy nourishment alone?
A fine way, this, thy time to fill!
The Doctor's in thy body still.
FAUST
What fresh and vital forces, canst thou guess,
Spring from my commerce with the wilderness?
But, if thou hadst the power of guessing,
Thou wouldst be devil enough to grudge my soul the blessing.
MEPHISTOPHELES
A blessing drawn from supernatural fountains!
In night and dew to lie upon the mountains;
All Heaven and Earth in rapture penetrating;
Thyself to Godhood haughtily inflating;
To grub with yearning force through Earth's dark marrow,
Compress the six days' work within thy bosom narrow,—
To taste, I know not what, in haughty power,
Thine own ecstatic life on all things shower,

111

Thine earthly self behind thee cast,
And then the lofty instinct, thus—
(With a gesture:)
at last,—
I daren't say how—to pluck the final flower!
FAUST
Shame on thee!
MEPHISTOPHELES
Yes, thou findest that unpleasant!
Thou hast the moral right to cry me "shame!" at present.
One dares not that before chaste ears declare,
Which chaste hearts, notwithstanding, cannot spare;
And, once for all, I grudge thee not the pleasure
Of lying to thyself in moderate measure.
But such a course thou wilt not long endure;
Already art thou o'er-excited,
And, if it last, wilt soon be plighted
To madness and to horror, sure.
Enough of that! Thy love sits lonely yonder,
By all things saddened and oppressed;
Her thoughts and yearnings seek thee, tenderer, fonder,—
mighty love is in her breast.
First came thy passion's flood and poured around her
As when from melted snow a streamlet overflows;
Thou hast therewith so filled and drowned her,
That now thy stream all shallow shows.
Methinks, instead of in the forests lording,
The noble Sir should find it good,
The love of this young silly blood
At once to set about rewarding.
Her time is miserably long;
She haunts her window, watching clouds that stray
O'er the old city-wall, and far away.
"Were I a little bird!" so runs her song,
Day long, and half night long.
Now she is lively, mostly sad,
Now, wept beyond her tears;
Then again quiet she appears,—Always
love-mad.
FAUST
Serpent! Serpent!
MEPHISTOPHELES (aside)
Ha! do I trap thee!
FAUST

Get thee away with thine offences,
Reprobate! Name not that fairest thing,
Nor the desire for her sweet body bring
Again before my half-distracted senses!
MEPHISTOPHELES
What wouldst thou, then? She thinks that thou art flown;
And half and half thou art, I own.
FAUST
Yet am I near, and love keeps watch and ward;
Though I were ne'er so far, it cannot falter:
I envy even the Body of the Lord
The touching of her lips, before the altar.
MEPHISTOPHELES
'Tis very well! My envy oft reposes
On your twin-pair, that feed among the roses.
FAUST
Away, thou pimp!
MEPHISTOPHELES
You rail, and it is fun to me.
The God, who fashioned youth and maid,
Perceived the noblest purpose of His trade,
And also made their opportunity.
Go on! It is a woe profound!
'Tis for your sweetheart's room you're bound,
And not for death, indeed.
FAUST
What are, within her arms, the heavenly blisses?
Though I be glowing with her kisses,
Do I not always share her need?
I am the fugitive, all houseless roaming,
The monster without air or rest,
That like a cataract, down rocks and gorges foaming,
Leaps, maddened, into the abyss's breast!
And side-wards she, with young unwakened senses,
Within her cabin on the Alpine field
Her simple, homely life commences,
Her little world therein concealed.
And I, God's hate flung o'er me,
Had not enough, to thrust
The stubborn rocks before me
And strike them into dust!
She and her peace I yet must undermine:
Thou, Hell, hast claimed this sacrifice as thine!
Help, Devil! through the coming pangs to push me;

What must be, let it quickly be!
Let fall on me her fate, and also crush me,—
One ruin whelm both her and me!
MEPHISTOPHELES
Again it seethes, again it glows!
Thou fool, go in and comfort her!
When such a head as thine no outlet knows,
It thinks the end must soon occur.
Hail him, who keeps a steadfast mind!
Thou, else, dost well the devil-nature wear:
Naught so insipid in the world I find
As is a devil in despair.
  Faust

XV

MARGARET'S ROOM

MARGARET
(at the spinning-wheel, alone)
My peace is gone,
My heart is sore:
I never shall find it,
Ah, nevermore!
Save I have him near.
The grave is here;
The world is gall
And bitterness all.
My poor weak head
Is racked and crazed;
My thought is lost,
My senses mazed.
My peace is gone,
My heart is sore:
I never shall find it,
Ah, nevermore!
To see him, him only,
At the pane I sit;
To meet him, him only,
The house I quit.
His lofty gait,
His noble size,
The smile of his mouth,
The power of his eyes,
And the magic flow
Of his talk, the bliss
In the clasp of his hand,
And, ah! his kiss!
My peace is gone,
My heart is sore:
I never shall find it,
Ah, nevermore!
My bosom yearns
For him alone;
Ah, dared I clasp him,
And hold, and own!
And kiss his mouth,
To heart's desire,

And on his kisses
At last expire!
 Faust

XVI

MARTHA'S GARDEN
MARGARET FAUST

MARGARET
Promise me, Henry!—
FAUST
What I can!
MARGARET
How is't with thy religion, pray?
Thou art a dear, good-hearted man,
And yet, I think, dost not incline that way.
FAUST
Leave that, my child! Thou know'st my love is tender;
For love, my blood and life would I surrender,
And as for Faith and Church, I grant to each his own.
MARGARET
That's not enough: we must believe thereon.
FAUST
Must we?
MARGARET
Would that I had some influence!
Then, too, thou honorest not the Holy Sacraments.
FAUST
I honor them.
MARGARET
Desiring no possession
'Tis long since thou hast been to mass or to confession.
Believest thou in God?
FAUST
My darling, who shall dare
"I believe in God!" to say?
Ask priest or sage the answer to declare,
And it will seem a mocking play,
A sarcasm on the asker.
MARGARET
Then thou believest not!
FAUST
Hear me not falsely, sweetest countenance!
Who dare express Him?
And who profess Him,
Saying: I believe in Him!
Who, feeling, seeing,

Deny His being,
Saying: I believe Him not!
The All-enfolding,
The All-upholding,
Folds and upholds he not
Thee, me, Himself?
Arches not there the sky above us?
Lies not beneath us, firm, the earth?
And rise not, on us shining,
Friendly, the everlasting stars?
Look I not, eye to eye, on thee,
And feel'st not, thronging
To head and heart, the force,
Still weaving its eternal secret,
Invisible, visible, round thy life?
Vast as it is, fill with that force thy heart,
And when thou in the feeling wholly blessed art,
Call it, then, what thou wilt,—
Call it Bliss! Heart! Love! God!
I have no name to give it!
Feeling is all in all:
The Name is sound and smoke,
Obscuring Heaven's clear glow.

MARGARET

All that is fine and good, to hear it so:
Much the same way the preacher spoke,
Only with slightly different phrases.

FAUST

The same thing, in all places,
All hearts that beat beneath the heavenly day—
Each in its language—say;
Then why not I, in mine, as well?

MARGARET

To hear it thus, it may seem passable;
And yet, some hitch in't there must be
For thou hast no Christianity.

FAUST

Dear love!

MARGARET

I've long been grieved to see
That thou art in such company.

FAUST

How so?

MARGARET

The man who with thee goes, thy mate,
Within my deepest, inmost soul I hate.
In all my life there's nothing
Has given my heart so keen a pang of loathing,
As his repulsive face has done.

FAUST

Nay, fear him not, my sweetest one!

MARGARET

I feel his presence like something ill.
I've else, for all, a kindly will,
But, much as my heart to see thee yearneth,
The secret horror of him returneth;
And I think the man a knave, as I live!
If I do him wrong, may God forgive!

FAUST

There must be such queer birds, however.

MARGARET

Live with the like of him, may I never!
When once inside the door comes he,
He looks around so sneeringly,
And half in wrath:
One sees that in nothing no interest he hath:
'Tis written on his very forehead
That love, to him, is a thing abhorréd.
I am so happy on thine arm,
So free, so yielding, and so warm,
And in his presence stifled seems my heart.

FAUST

Foreboding angel that thou art!

MARGARET

It overcomes me in such degree,
That wheresoe'er he meets us, even,
I feel as though I'd lost my love for thee.
When he is by, I could not pray to Heaven.
That burns within me like a flame,
And surely, Henry, 'tis with thee the same.

FAUST

There, now, is thine antipathy!

MARGARET

But I must go.

FAUST

Ah, shall there never be
A quiet hour, to see us fondly plighted,
With breast to breast, and soul to soul united?

MARGARET

Ah, if I only slept alone!
I'd draw the bolts to-night, for thy desire;
But mother's sleep so light has grown,
And if we were discovered by her,
'Twould be my death upon the spot!

FAUST

Thou angel, fear it not!
Here is a phial: in her drink
But three drops of it measure,
And deepest sleep will on her senses sink.

MARGARET

What would I not, to give thee pleasure?
It will not harm her, when one tries it?

FAUST

If 'twould, my love, would I advise it?

MARGARET

Ah, dearest man, if but thy face I see,
I know not what compels me to thy will:
So much have I already done for thee,
That scarcely more is left me to fulfil.
(Enter MEPHISTOPHELES.)   [Exit.

MEPHISTOPHELES

The monkey! Is she gone?

FAUST

Hast played the spy again?

MEPHISTOPHELES

I've heard, most fully, how she drew thee.
The Doctor has been catechised, 'tis plain;
Great good, I hope, the thing will do thee.
The girls have much desire to ascertain
If one is prim and good, as ancient rules compel:
If there he's led, they think, he'll follow them as well.

FAUST

Thou, monster, wilt nor see nor own
How this pure soul, of faith so lowly,
So loving and ineffable,—
The faith alone
That her salvation is,—with scruples holy
Pines, lest she hold as lost the man she loves so well!

MEPHISTOPHELES

Thou, full of sensual, super-sensual desire,
A girl by the nose is leading thee.

FAUST

Abortion, thou, of filth and fire!
MEPHISTOPHELES
And then, how masterly she reads physiognomy!
When I am present she's impressed, she knows not how;
She in my mask a hidden sense would read:
She feels that surely I'm a genius now,—
Perhaps the very Devil, indeed!
Well, well,—to-night—?
FAUST
What's that to thee?
MEPHISTOPHELES
Yet my delight 'twill also be!
 Faust

XVII

AT THE FOUNTAIN
MARGARET and LISBETH With pitchers.

LISBETH
Hast nothing heard of Barbara?
MARGARET
No, not a word. I go so little out.
LISBETH
It's true, Sibylla said, to-day.
She's played the fool at last, there's not a doubt.
Such taking-on of airs!
MARGARET
How so?

LISBETH
It stinks!
She's feeding two, whene'er she eats and drinks.
MARGARET
Ah!
LISBETH
    And so, at last, it serves her rightly.
She clung to the fellow so long and tightly!
That was a promenading!
At village and dance parading!
As the first they must everywhere shine,
And he treated her always to pies and wine,
And she made a to-do with her face so fine;
So mean and shameless was her behavior,
She took all the presents the fellow gave her.
'Twas kissing and coddling, on and on!
So now, at the end, the flower is gone.
MARGARET
The poor, poor thing!
LISBETH
Dost pity her, at that?
When one of us at spinning sat,
And mother, nights, ne'er let us out the door
She sported with her paramour.
On the door-bench, in the passage dark,
The length of the time they'd never mark.
So now her head no more she'll lift,
But do church-penance in her sinner's shift!

122

MARGARET

He'll surely take her for his wife.

LISBETH

He'd be a fool! A brisk young blade
Has room, elsewhere, to ply his trade.
Besides, he's gone.

MARGARET

That is not fair!

LISBETH

If him she gets, why let her beware!
The boys shall dash her wreath on the floor,
And we'll scatter chaff before her door!
[Exit.

MARGARET (returning home)

How scornfully I once reviled,
When some poor maiden was beguiled!
More speech than any tongue suffices
I craved, to censure others' vices.
Black as it seemed, I blackened still,
And blacker yet was in my will;
And blessed myself, and boasted high,—
And now—a living sin am I!
Yet—all that drove my heart thereto,
God! was so good, so dear, so true!

Faust

DONJON
(In a niche of the wall a shrine, with an image of the Mater Dolorosa. Pots of flowers before it.)

MARGARET
(putting fresh flowers in the pots)
Incline, O Maiden,
Thou sorrow-laden,
Thy gracious countenance upon my pain!
The sword Thy heart in,
With anguish smarting,
Thou lookest up to where Thy Son is slain!
Thou seest the Father;
Thy sad sighs gather,
And bear aloft Thy sorrow and His pain!
Ah, past guessing,
Beyond expressing,
The pangs that wring my flesh and bone!
Why this anxious heart so burneth,
Why it trembleth, why it yearneth,
Knowest Thou, and Thou alone!
Where'er I go, what sorrow,
What woe, what woe and sorrow
Within my bosom aches!
Alone, and ah! unsleeping,
I'm weeping, weeping, weeping,
The heart within me breaks.
The pots before my window,
Alas! my tears did wet,
As in the early morning
For thee these flowers I set.
Within my lonely chamber
The morning sun shone red:
I sat, in utter sorrow,
Already on my bed.
Help! rescue me from death and stain!
O Maiden!
Thou sorrow-laden,
Incline Thy countenance upon my pain!
  Faust

NIGHT
STREET BEFORE MARGARET'S DOOR

VALENTINE (a soldier, MARGARET'S brother)
When I have sat at some carouse.
Where each to each his brag allows,
And many a comrade praised to me
His pink of girls right lustily,
With brimming glass that spilled the toast,
And elbows planted as in boast:
I sat in unconcerned repose,
And heard the swagger as it rose.
And stroking then my beard, I'd say,
Smiling, the bumper in my hand:
"Each well enough in her own way.
But is there one in all the land
Like sister Margaret, good as gold,—
One that to her can a candle hold?"
Cling! clang! "Here's to her!" went around
The board: "He speaks the truth!" cried some;
"In her the flower o' the sex is found!"
And all the swaggerers were dumb.
And now!—I could tear my hair with vexation.
And dash out my brains in desperation!
With turned-up nose each scamp may face me,
With sneers and stinging taunts disgrace me,
And, like a bankrupt debtor sitting,
A chance-dropped word may set me sweating!
Yet, though I thresh them all together,
I cannot call them liars, either.
But what comes sneaking, there, to view?
If I mistake not, there are two.
If he's one, let me at him drive!
He shall not leave the spot alive.
FAUST MEPHISTOPHELES
FAUST
How from the window of the sacristy
Upward th'eternal lamp sends forth a glimmer,
That, lessening side-wards, fainter grows and dimmer,
Till darkness closes from the sky!
The shadows thus within my bosom gather.

125

MEPHISTOPHELES

I'm like a sentimental tom-cat, rather,
That round the tall fire-ladders sweeps,
And stealthy, then, along the coping creeps:
Quite virtuous, withal, I come,
A little thievish and a little frolicsome.
I feel in every limb the presage
Forerunning the grand Walpurgis-Night:
Day after to-morrow brings its message,
And one keeps watch then with delight.

FAUST

Meanwhile, may not the treasure risen be,
Which there, behind, I glimmering see?

MEPHISTOPHELES

Shalt soon experience the pleasure,
To lift the kettle with its treasure.
I lately gave therein a squint—
Saw splendid lion-dollars in 't.

FAUST

Not even a jewel, not a ring,
To deck therewith my darling girl?

MEPHISTOPHELES

I saw, among the rest, a thing
That seemed to be a chain of pearl.

FAUST

That's well, indeed! For painful is it
To bring no gift when her I visit.

MEPHISTOPHELES

Thou shouldst not find it so annoying,
Without return to be enjoying.
Now, while the sky leads forth its starry throng,
Thou'lt hear a masterpiece, no work completer:
I'll sing her, first, a moral song,
The surer, afterwards, to cheat her.
(Sings to the cither.)
What dost thou here
In daybreak clear,
Kathrina dear,
Before thy lover's door?
Beware! the blade
Lets in a maid.
That out a maid
Departeth nevermore!
The coaxing shun

Of such an one!
When once 'tis done
Good-night to thee, poor thing!
Love's time is brief:
Unto no thief
Be warm and lief,
But with the wedding-ring!
VALENTINE (comes forward)
Whom wilt thou lure? God's-element!
Rat-catching piper, thou!—perdition!
To the Devil, first, the instrument!
To the Devil, then, the curst musician!
MEPHISTOPHELES
The cither's smashed! For nothing more 'tis fitting.
VALENTINE
There's yet a skull I must be splitting!
MEPHISTOPHELES (to FAUST)
Sir Doctor, don't retreat, I pray!
Stand by: I'll lead, if you'll but tarry:
Out with your spit, without delay!
You've but to lunge, and I will parry.
VALENTINE
Then parry that!
MEPHISTOPHELES
Why not? 'tis light.
VALENTINE
That, too!
MEPHISTOPHELES
Of course.
VALENTINE
I think the Devil must fight!
How is it, then? my hand's already lame:
MEPHISTOPHELES (to FAUST)
Thrust home!
VALENTINE (jails)
O God!
MEPHISTOPHELES
Now is the lubber tame!
But come, away! 'Tis time for us to fly;
For there arises now a murderous cry.
With the police 'twere easy to compound it,
But here the penal court will sift and sound it.
[Exit with FAUST.
MARTHA (at the window)

Come out! Come out!

MARGARET (at the window)

Quick, bring a light!

MARTHA (as above)

They swear and storm, they yell and fight!

PEOPLE

Here lies one dead already—see!

MARTHA (coming from the house)

The murderers, whither have they run?

MARGARET (coming out)

Who lies here?

PEOPLE

'Tis thy mother's son!

MARGARET

Almighty God! what misery!

VALENTINE

I'm dying! That is quickly said,
And quicker yet 'tis done.
Why howl, you women there? Instead,
Come here and listen, every one!
(All gather around him)
My Margaret, see! still young thou art,
But not the least bit shrewd or smart,
Thy business thus to slight:
So this advice I bid thee heed—
Now that thou art a whore indeed,
Why, be one then, outright!

MARGARET

My brother! God! such words to me?

VALENTINE

In this game let our Lord God be!
What's done's already done, alas!
What follows it, must come to pass.
With one begin'st thou secretly,
Then soon will others come to thee,
And when a dozen thee have known,
Thou'rt also free to all the town.
When Shame is born and first appears,
She is in secret brought to light,
And then they draw the veil of night
Over her head and ears;
Her life, in fact, they're loath to spare her.
But let her growth and strength display,
She walks abroad unveiled by day,

Yet is not grown a whit the fairer.
The uglier she is to sight,
The more she seeks the day's broad light.
The time I verily can discern
When all the honest folk will turn
From thee, thou jade! and seek protection
As from a corpse that breeds infection.
Thy guilty heart shall then dismay thee.
When they but look thee in the face:—
Shalt not in a golden chain array thee,
Nor at the altar take thy place!
Shalt not, in lace and ribbons flowing,
Make merry when the dance is going!
But in some corner, woe betide thee!
Among the beggars and cripples hide thee;
And so, though even God forgive,
On earth a damned existence live!
MARTHA
Commend your soul to God for pardon,
That you your heart with slander harden!
VALENTINE
Thou pimp most infamous, be still!
Could I thy withered body kill,
'Twould bring, for all my sinful pleasure,
Forgiveness in the richest measure.
MARGARET
My brother! This is Hell's own pain!
VALENTINE
I tell thee, from thy tears refrain!
When thou from honor didst depart
It stabbed me to the very heart.
Now through the slumber of the grave
I go to God as a soldier brave.
(Dies.)
Faust

XX
CATHEDRAL
SERVICE, ORGAN and ANTHEM.
(MARGARET among much people: the EVIL SPIRIT behind
MARGARET.)

EVIL SPIRIT
HOW otherwise was it, Margaret,
When thou, still innocent,
Here to the altar cam'st,
And from the worn and fingered book
Thy prayers didst prattle,
Half sport of childhood,
Half God within thee!
Margaret!
Where tends thy thought?
Within thy bosom
What hidden crime?
Pray'st thou for mercy on thy mother's soul,
That fell asleep to long, long torment, and through thee?
Upon thy threshold whose the blood?
And stirreth not and quickens
Something beneath thy heart,
Thy life disquieting
With most foreboding presence?
MARGARET
Woe! woe!
Would I were free from the thoughts
That cross me, drawing hither and thither
Despite me!
CHORUS
Diesira, dies illa,
Solvet soeclum in favilla!
(Sound of the organ.)
EVIL SPIRIT
Wrath takes thee!
The trumpet peals!
The graves tremble!
And thy heart
From ashy rest
To fiery torments
Now again requickened,
Throbs to life!

MARGARET
Would I were forth!
I feel as if the organ here
My breath takes from me,
My very heart
Dissolved by the anthem!
CHORUS
Judex ergo cum sedebit,
Quidquid latet, ad parebit,
Nil inultum remanebit.
MARGARET
I cannot breathe!
The massy pillars
Imprison me!
The vaulted arches
Crush me!—Air!
EVIL SPIRIT
Hide thyself! Sin and shame
Stay never hidden.
Air? Light?
Woe to thee!
CHORUS
Quid sum miser tunc dicturus,
Quem patronem rogaturus,
Cum vix Justus sit securus
EVIL SPIRIT
They turn their faces,
The glorified, from thee:
The pure, their hands to offer,
Shuddering, refuse thee!
Woe!
CHORUS
Quid sum miser tune dicturus?
MARGARET
Neighbor! your cordial!   (She falls in a swoon.)

XXI
WALPURGIS-NIGHT
THE HARTZ MOUNTAINS.
District of Schierke and Elend.
FAUST MEPHISTOPHELES

MEPHISTOPHELES
DOST thou not wish a broomstick-steed's assistance?
The sturdiest he-goat I would gladly see:
The way we take, our goal is yet some distance.
FAUST
So long as in my legs I feel the fresh existence.
This knotted staff suffices me.
What need to shorten so the way?
Along this labyrinth of vales to wander,
Then climb the rocky ramparts yonder,
Wherefrom the fountain flings eternal spray,
Is such delight, my steps would fain delay.
The spring-time stirs within the fragrant birches,
And even the fir-tree feels it now:
Should then our limbs escape its gentle searches?
MEPHISTOPHELES
I notice no such thing, I vow!
'Tis winter still within my body:
Upon my path I wish for frost and snow.
How sadly rises, incomplete and ruddy,
The moon's lone disk, with its belated glow,
And lights so dimly, that, as one advances,
At every step one strikes a rock or tree!
Let us, then, use a Jack-o'-lantern's glances:
I see one yonder, burning merrily.
Ho, there! my friend! I'll levy thine attendance:
Why waste so vainly thy resplendence?
Be kind enough to light us up the steep!
WILL-O'-THE-WISP
My reverence, I hope, will me enable
To curb my temperament unstable;
For zigzag courses we are wont to keep.
MEPHISTOPHELES
Indeed? he'd like mankind to imitate!
Now, in the Devil's name, go straight,
Or I'll blow out his being's flickering spark!
WILL-O'-THE-WISP

You are the master of the house, I mark,
And I shall try to serve you nicely.
But then, reflect: the mountain's magic-mad to-day,
And if a will-o'-the-wisp must guide you on the way,
You mustn't take things too precisely.
FAUST, MEPHISTOPHELES, WILL-O'-THE-WISP
(in alternating song)
We, it seems, have entered newly
In the sphere of dreams enchanted.
Do thy bidding, guide us truly,
That our feet be forwards planted
In the vast, the desert spaces!
See them swiftly changing places,
Trees on trees beside us trooping,
And the crags above us stooping,
And the rocky snouts, outgrowing,—
Hear them snoring, hear them blowing!
O'er the stones, the grasses, flowing
Stream and streamlet seek the hollow.
Hear I noises? songs that follow?
Hear I tender love-petitions?
Voices of those heavenly visions?
Sounds of hope, of love undying!
And the echoes, like traditions
Of old days, come faint and hollow.
Hoo-hoo! Shoo-hoo! Nearer hover
Jay and screech-owl, and the plover,—
Are they all awake and crying?
Is't the salamander pushes,
Bloated-bellied, through the bushes?
And the roots, like serpents twisted,
Through the sand and boulders toiling,
Fright us, weirdest links uncoiling
To entrap us, unresisted:
Living knots and gnarls uncanny
Feel with polypus-antennae
For the wanderer. Mice are flying,
Thousand-colored, herd-wise hieing
Through the moss and through the heather!
And the fire-flies wink and darkle,
Crowded swarms that soar and sparkle,
And in wildering escort gather!
Tell me, if we still are standing,
Or if further we're ascending?

133

All is turning, whirling, blending,
Trees and rocks with grinning faces,
Wandering lights that spin in mazes,
Still increasing and expanding!
MEPHISTOPHELES
Grasp my skirt with heart undaunted!
Here a middle-peak is planted,
Whence one seeth, with amaze,
Mammon in the mountain blaze.
FAUST
How strangely glimmers through the hollows
A dreary light, like that of dawn!
Its exhalation tracks and follows
The deepest gorges, faint and wan.
Here steam, there rolling vapor sweepeth;
Here burns the glow through film and haze:
Now like a tender thread it creepeth,
Now like a fountain leaps and plays.
Here winds away, and in a hundred
Divided veins the valley braids:
There, in a corner pressed and sundered,
Itself detaches, spreads and fades.
Here gush the sparkles incandescent
Like scattered showers of golden sand;—
But, see! in all their height, at present,
The rocky ramparts blazing stand.

Under the old ribs of the rock retreating

Under the old ribs of the rock retreating
MEPHISTOPHELES
Has not Sir Mammon grandly lighted
His palace for this festal night?
'Tis lucky thou hast seen the sight;
The boisterous guests approach that were invited.
FAUST
How raves the tempest through the air!
With what fierce blows upon my neck 'tis beating!
MEPHISTOPHELES
Under the old ribs of the rock retreating,
Hold fast, lest thou be hurled·down the abysses there!
The night with the mist is black;
Hark! how the forests grind and crack!
Frightened, the owlets are scattered:

Hearken! the pillars are shattered.
The evergreen palaces shaking!
Boughs are groaning and breaking,
The tree-trunks terribly thunder,
The roots are twisting asunder!
In frightfully intricate crashing
Each on the other is dashing,
And over the wreck-strewn gorges
The tempest whistles and surges!
Hear'st thou voices higher ringing?
Far away, or nearer singing?
Yes, the mountain's side along,
Sweeps an infuriate glamouring song!
WITCHES (in chorus)
The witches ride to the Brocken's top,
The stubble is yellow, and green the crop.
There gathers the crowd for carnival:
Sir Urian sits over all.
And so they go over stone and stock;
The witch she——s, and——s the buck.
A VOICE
Alone, old Baubo's coming now;
She rides upon a farrow-sow.
CHORUS
Then honor to whom the honor is due!
Dame Baubo first, to lead the crew!
A tough old sow and the mother thereon,
Then follow the witches, every one.
A VOICE
Which way com'st thou hither?
VOICE
O'er the Ilsen-stone.
I peeped at the owl in her nest alone:
How she stared and glared!
VOICE
Betake thee to Hell!
Why so fast and so fell?
VOICE
She has scored and has flayed me:
See the wounds she has made me!
WITCHES (chorus)
The way is wide, the way is long:
See, what a wild and crazy throng!
The broom it scratches, the fork it thrusts,

135

The child is stifled, the mother bursts.
WIZARDS (semichorus)
As doth the snail in shell, we crawl:
Before us go the women all.
When towards the Devil's House we tread,
Woman's a thousand steps ahead.
OTHER SEMICHORUS
We do not measure with such care:
Woman in thousand steps is theft.
But howsoe'er she hasten may,
Man in one leap has cleared the way.
VOICE (from above)
Come on, come on, from Rocky Lake!
VOICE (from below)
Aloft we'd fain ourselves betake.
We've washed, and are bright as ever you will,
Yet we're eternally sterile still.
BOTH CHORUSES
The wind is hushed, the star shoots by.
The dreary moon forsakes the sky;
The magic notes, like spark on spark,
Drizzle, whistling through the dark.
VOICE (from below)
Halt, there! Ho, there!
VOICE (from above)
Who calls from the rocky cleft below there?
VOICE (below)
Take me, too! take me, too!
I'm climbing now three hundred years,
And yet the summit cannot see:
Among my equals I would be.
BOTH CHORUSES
Bears the broom and bears the stock,
Bears the fork and bears the buck:
Who cannot raise himself to-night
Is evermore a ruined wight.
HALF-WITCH (below)
So long I stumble, ill bestead,
And the others are now so far ahead!
At home I've neither rest nor cheer,
And yet I cannot gain them here.
CHORUS OF WITCHES
To cheer the witch will salve avail;
A rag will answer for a sail;

Each trough a goodly ship supplies;
He ne'er will fly, who now not flies.
BOTH CHORUSES
When round the summit whirls our flight,
Then lower, and on the ground alight;
And far and wide the heather press
With witchhood's swarms of wantonness!
(They settle down.)
MEPHISTOPHELES
They crowd and push, they roar and clatter!
They whirl and whistle, pull and chatter!
They shine, and spirt, and stink, and burn!
The true witch-element we learn.
Keep close! or we are parted, in our turn,
Where art thou?
FAUST (in the distance)
Here!
MEPHISTOPHELES
What! whirled so far astray?
Then house-right I must use, and clear the way.
Make room! Squire Voland comes! Room, gentle rabble,
room!
Here, Doctor, hold to me: in one jump we'll resume
An easier space, and from the crowd be free:
It's too much, even for the like of me.
Yonder, with special light, there's something shining clearer
Within those bushes; I've a mind to see.
Come on! well slip a little nearer.
FAUST
Spirit of Contradiction! On! I'll follow straight.
'Tis planned most wisely, if I judge aright:
We climb the Brocken's top in the Walpurgis-Night,
That arbitrarily, here, ourselves we isolate.
MEPHISTOPHELES
But see, what motley flames among the heather!
There is a lively club together:
In smaller circles one is not alone.
FAUST
Better the summit, I must own:
There fire and whirling smoke I see.
They seek the Evil One in wild confusion:
Many enigmas there might find solution.
MEPHISTOPHELES
But there enigmas also knotted be.

137

Leave to the multitude their riot!
Here will we house ourselves in quiet.
It is an old, transmitted trade,
That in the greater world the little worlds are made.
I see stark-nude young witches congregate,
And old ones, veiled and hidden shrewdly:
On my account be kind, nor treat them rudely!
The trouble's small, the fun is great.
I hear the noise of instruments attuning,—
Vile din! yet one must learn to bear the crooning.
Come, come along! It must be, I declare!
I'll go ahead and introduce thee there,
Thine obligation newly earning.
That is no little space: what say'st thou, friend?
Look yonder! thou canst scarcely see the end:
A hundred fires along the ranks are burning.
They dance, they chat, they cook, they drink, they court:
Now where, just tell me, is there better sport?

FAUST

Wilt thou, to introduce us to the revel,
Assume the part of wizard or of devil?

MEPHISTOPHELES

I'm mostly used, 'tis true, to go incognito,
But on a gala-day one may his orders show.
The Garter does not deck my suit,
But honored and at home is here the cloven foot.
Perceiv'st thou yonder snail? It cometh, slow and steady;
So delicately its feelers pry,
That it hath scented me already:
I cannot here disguise me, if I try.
But come! we'll go from this fire to a newer:
I am the go-between, and thou the wooer.
(To some, who are sitting around dying embers:)
Old gentlemen, why at the outskirts? Enter!
I'd praise you if I found you snugly in the centre,
With youth and revel round you like a zone:
You each, at home, are quite enough alone.

GENERAL

Say, who would put his trust in nations,
Howe'er for them one may have worked and planned?
For with the people, as with women,
Youth always has the upper hand.

MINISTER

They're now too far from what is just and sage.

I praise the old ones, not unduly:
When we were all-in-all, then, truly,
Then was the real golden age.
PARVENU
We also were not stupid, either,
And what we should not, often did;
But now all things have from their bases slid,
Just as we meant to hold them fast together.
AUTHOR
Who, now, a work of moderate sense will read?
Such works are held as antiquate and mossy;
And as regards the younger folk, indeed,
They never yet have been so pert and saucy.
MEPHISTOPHELES
(who all at once appears very old)
I feel that men are ripe for Judgment-Day,
Now for the last time I've the witches'-hill ascended:
Since to the lees my cask is drained away,
The world's, as well, must soon be ended.
HUCKSTER-WITCH
Ye gentlemen, don't pass me thus!
Let not the chance neglected be!
Behold my wares attentively:
The stock is rare and various.
And yet, there's nothing I've collected—
No shop, on earth, like this you'll find!—
Which has not, once, sore hurt inflicted
Upon the world, and on mankind.
No dagger's here, that set not blood to flowing;
No cup, that hath not once, within a healthy frame
Poured speedy death, in poison glowing:
No gems, that have not brought a maid to shame;
No sword, but severed ties for the unwary,
Or from behind struck down the adversary.
MEPHISTOPHELES
Gossip! the times thou badly comprehendest:
What's done has happed—what haps, is done!
'Twere better if for novelties thou sendest:
By such alone can we be won.
FAUST
Let me not lose myself in all this pother!
This is a fair, as never was another!
MEPHISTOPHELES
The whirlpool swirls to get above:

Thou'rt shoved thyself, imagining to shove.
FAUST
But who is that?
MEPHISTOPHELES
Note her especially,
Tis Lilith.
FAUST
Who?
MEPHISTOPHELES
Adam's first wife is she.
Beware the lure within her lovely tresses,
The splendid sole adornment of her hair!
When she succeeds therewith a youth to snare,
Not soon again she frees him from her jesses.
FAUST
Those two, the old one with the young one sitting,
They've danced already more than fitting.
MEPHISTOPHELES
No rest to-night for young or old!
They start another dance: come now, let us take hold!
FAUST (dancing with the young witch)
A lovely dream once came to me;
I then beheld an apple-tree,
And there two fairest apples shone:
They lured me so, I climbed thereon.
THE FAIR ONE
Apples have been desired by you,
Since first in Paradise they grew;
And I am moved with joy, to know
That such within my garden grow.
MEPHISTOPHELES (dancing with the old one)
A dissolute dream once came to me:
Therein I saw a cloven tree,
Which had a————————;
Yet,——as 'twas, I fancied it.
THE OLD ONE
I offer here my best salute
Unto the knight with cloven foot!
Let him a————————prepare,
If him————————————does not scare.
PROKTOPHANTASMIST
Accurséd folk! How dare you venture thus?
Had you not, long since, demonstration
That ghosts can't stand on ordinary foundation?

And now you even dance, like one of us!
THE FAIR ONE (dancing)
Why does he come, then, to our ball?
FAUST (dancing)
O, everywhere on him you fall!
When others dance, he weighs the matter:
If he can't every step bechatter,
Then 'tis the same as were the step not made;
But if you forwards go, his ire is most displayed.
If you would whirl in regular gyration
As he does in his dull old mill,
He'd show, at any rate, good-will,—
Especially if you heard and heeded his hortation.
PROKTOPHANTASMIST
You still are here? Nay, 'tis a thing unheard!
Vanish, at once! We've said the enlightening word.
The pack of devils by no rules is daunted:
We are so wise, and yet is Tegel haunted.
To clear the folly out, how have I swept and stirred!
Twill ne'er be clean: why, 'tis a thing unheard!
THE FAIR ONE
Then cease to bore us at our ball!
PROKTOPHANTASMIST
I tell you, spirits, to your face,
I give to spirit-despotism no place;
My spirit cannot practise it at all.
(The dance continues)
Naught will succeed, I see, amid such revels;
Yet something from a tour I always save,
And hope, before my last step to the grave,
To overcome the poets and the devils.
MEPHISTOPHELES
He now will seat him in the nearest puddle;
The solace this, whereof he's most assured:
And when upon his rump the leeches hang and fuddle,
He'll be of spirits and of Spirit cured.
(To FAUST, who has left the dance:)
Wherefore forsakest thou the lovely maiden,
That in the dance so sweetly sang?
FAUST
Ah! in the midst of it there sprang
A red mouse from her mouth—sufficient reason.
MEPHISTOPHELES
That's nothing! One must not so squeamish be;

So the mouse was not gray, enough for thee.
Who'd think of that in love's selected season?
FAUST
Then saw I—.
MEPHISTOPHELES
What?
FAUST
Mephisto, seest thou there,
Alone and far, a girl most pale and fair?
She falters on, her way scarce knowing,
As if with fettered feet that stay her going.
I must confess, it seems to me
As if my kindly Margaret were she.
MEPHISTOPHELES
Let the thing be! All thence have evil drawn:
It is a magic shape, a lifeless eidolon.
Such to encounter is not good:
Their blank, set stare benumbs the human blood,
And one is almost turned to stone.
Medusa's tale to thee is known.
FAUST
Forsooth, the eyes they are of one whom, dying,
No hand with loving pressure closed;
That is the breast whereon I once was lying,—
The body sweet, beside which I reposed!
MEPHISTOPHELES
Tis magic all, thou fool, seduced so easily!
Unto each man his love she seems to be.
FAUST
The woe, the rapture, so ensnare me,
That from her gaze I cannot tear me!
And, strange! around her fairest throat
A single scarlet band is gleaming,
No broader than a knife-blade seeming!
MEPHISTOPHELES
Quite right! The mark I also note.
Her head beneath her arm she'll sometimes carry;
Twas Perseus lopped it, her old adversary.
Thou crav'st the same illusion still!
Come, let us mount this little hill;
The Prater shows no livelier stir,
And, if they've not bewitched my sense,
I verily see a theatre.
What's going on?

142

SERVIBILIS

'Twill shortly recommence:
A new performance—'tis the last of seven.
To give that number is the custom here:
'Twas by a Dilettante written,
And Dilettanti in the parts appear.
That now I vanish, pardon, I entreat you!
As Dilettante I the curtain raise.

MEPHISTOPHELES

When I upon the Blocksberg meet you,
I find it good: for that's your proper place.

 Faust

XXII

WALPURGIS-NIGHT'S DREAM
OBERON AND TITANIA's GOLDEN WEDDING
INTERMEZZO

MANAGER
Sons of Mieding, rest to-day!
Needless your machinery:
Misty vale and mountain gray,
That is all the scenery.
HERALD
That the wedding golden be.
Must fifty years be rounded:
But the Golden give to me,
When the strife's compounded.
OBERON
Spirits, if you're here, be seen—
Show yourselves, delighted!
Fairy king and fairy queen,
They are newly plighted.
PUCK
Cometh Puck, and, light of limb,
Whisks and whirls in measure:
Come a hundred after him,
To share with him the pleasure.
ARIEL
Ariel's song is heavenly-pure,
His tones are sweet and rare ones:
Though ugly faces he allure,
Yet he allures the fair ones.
OBERON
Spouses, who would fain agree,
Learn how we were mated!
If your pairs would loving be,
First be separated!
TITANIA
If her whims the wife control,
And the man berate her,
Take him to the Northern Pole,
And her to the Equator!
ORCHESTRA. TUTTI.
Fortissimo.
Snout of fly, mosquito-bill,

144

And kin of all conditions,
Frog in grass, and cricket-trill,—
These are the musicians!
SOLO
See the bagpipe on our track!
'Tis the soap-blown bubble:
Hear the schnecke-schnicke-schnack
Through his nostrils double!
SPIRIT, JUST GROWING INTO FORM
Spider's foot and paunch of toad,
And little wings—we know 'em!
A little creature 'twill not be,
But yet, a little poem.
A LITTLE COUPLE
Little step and lofty leap
Through honey-dew and fragrance:
You'll never mount the airy steep
With all your tripping vagrance.
INQUISITIVE TRAVELLER
Is't but masquerading play?
See I with precision?
Oberon, the beauteous fay,
Meets, to-night, my vision!
ORTHODOX
Not a claw, no tail I see!
And yet, beyond a cavil,
Like "the Gods of Greece," must he
Also be a devil.
NORTHERN ARTIST
I only seize, with sketchy air,
Some outlines of the tourney;
Yet I betimes myself prepare
For my Italian journey.
PURIST
My bad luck brings me here, alas!
How roars the orgy louder!
And of the witches in the mass,
But only two wear powder.
YOUNG WITCH
Powder becomes, like petticoat,
A gray and wrinkled noddy;
So I sit naked on my goat,
And show a strapping body.
MATRON

We've too much tact and policy
To rate with gibes a scolder;
Yet, young and tender though you be,
I hope to see you moulder.
LEADER OF THE BAND
Fly-snout and mosquito-bill,
Don't swarm so round the Naked!
Frog in grass and cricket-trill,
Observe the time, and make it!
WEATHERCOCK (towards one side)
Society to one's desire!
Brides only, and the sweetest!
And bachelors of youth and fire.
And prospects the completest!
WEATHERCOCK (towards the other side)
And if the Earth don't open now
To swallow up each ranter,
Why, then will I myself, I vow,
Jump into hell instanter!
XENIES
Us as little insects see!
With sharpest nippers flitting,
That our Papa Satan we
May honor as is fitting.
HENNINGS
How, in crowds together massed,
They are jesting, shameless!
They will even say, at last,
That their hearts are blameless.
MUSAGETES
Among this witches' revelry
His way one gladly loses;
And, truly, it would easier be
Than to command the Muses.
CI-DEVANT GENIUS OF THE AGE
The proper folks one's talents laud:
Come on, and none shall pass us!
The Blocksberg has a summit broad,
Like Germany's Parnassus.
INQUISITIVE TRAVELLER
Say, who's the stiff and pompous man?
He walks with haughty paces:
He snuffles all he snuffle can:
"He scents the Jesuits' traces."

CRANE
Both clear and muddy streams, for me
Are good to fish and sport in:
And thus the pious man you see
With even devils consorting.
WORLDLING
Yes, for the pious, I suspect,
All instruments are fitting;
And on the Blocksberg they erect
Full many a place of meeting.
DANCER
A newer chorus now succeeds!
I hear the distant drumming.
"Don't be disturbed! 'tis, in the reeds,
The bittern's changeless booming."
DANCING-MASTER
How each his legs in nimble trip
Lifts up, and makes a clearance!
The crooked jump, the heavy skip,
Nor care for the appearance.
GOOD FELLOW
The rabble by such hate are held,
To maim and slay delights them:
As Orpheus' lyre the brutes compelled,
The bagpipe here unites them.
DOGMATIST
I'll not be led by any lure
Of doubts or critic-cavils:
The Devil must be something, sure,—
Or how should there be devils?
IDEALIST
This once, the fancy wrought in me
Is really too despotic:
Forsooth, if I am all I see,
I must be idiotic!
REALIST
This racking fuss on every hand,
It gives me great vexation;
And, for the first time, here I stand
On insecure foundation.
SUPERNATURALIST
With much delight I see the play,
And grant to these their merits,
Since from the devils I also may

147

Infer the better spirits.
SCEPTIC
The flame they follow, on and on,
And think they're near the treasure:
But Devil rhymes with Doubt alone,
So I am here with pleasure.
LEADER OF THE BAND
Frog in green, and cricket-trill.
Such dilettants!—perdition!
Fly-snout and mosquito-bill,—
Each one's a fine musician!
THE ADROIT
Sans souci, we call the clan
Of merry creatures so, then;
Go a-foot no more we can,
And on our heads we go, then.
THE AWKWARD
Once many a bit we sponged, but now,
God help us! that is done with:
Our shoes are all danced out, we trow,
We've but naked soles to run with.
WILL-O'-THE WISPS
From the marshes we appear,
Where we originated;
Yet in the ranks, at once, we're here
As glittering gallants rated.
SHOOTING-STAR
Darting hither from the sky,
In star and fire light shooting,
Cross-wise now in grass I lie:
Who'll help me to my footing?
THE HEAVY FELLOWS
Room! and round about us, room!
Trodden are the grasses:
Spirits also, spirits come,
And they are bulky masses.
PUCK
Enter not so stall-fed quite,
Like elephant-calves about one!
And the heaviest weight to-night
Be Puck, himself, the stout one!
ARIEL
If loving Nature at your back,
Or Mind, the wings uncloses,

Follow up my airy track
To the mount of roses!
ORCHESTRA
pianissimo
Cloud and trailing mist o'erhead
Are now illuminated:
Air in leaves, and wind in reed,
And all is dissipated.

XXIII
DREARY DAY
A FIELD
FAUST MEPHISTOPHELES

FAUST

In misery! In despair! Long wretchedly astray on the face
of the earth, and now imprisoned! That gracious, ill-starred
creature shut in a dungeon as a criminal, and given
up to fearful torments! To this has it come! to this!—Treacherous,
contemptible spirit, and thou hast concealed it from
me!—Stand, then,—stand! Roll the devilish eyes wrathfully in
thy head! Stand and defy me with thine intolerable presence!
Imprisoned! In irretrievable misery! Delivered up to evil
spirits, and to condemning, unfeeling Man! And thou hast
lulled me, meanwhile, with the most insipid dissipations, hast
concealed from me her increasing wretchedness, and suffered
her to go helplessly to ruin!
  Roll the devilish eyes wrathfully in thy head
Roll the devilish eyes wrathfully in thy head
MEPHISTOPHELES
She is not the first.
FAUST
Dog! Abominable monster! Transform him, thou Infinite
Spirit! transform the reptile again into his dog-shape? in which
it pleased him often at night to scamper on before me, to roll
himself at the feet of the unsuspecting wanderer, and hang
upon his shoulders when he fell! Transform him again into
his favorite likeness, that he may crawl upon his belly in the
dust before me,—that I may trample him, the outlawed, under
foot! Not the first! O woe! woe which no human soul can
grasp, that more than one being should sink into the depths
of this misery,—that the first, in its writhing death-agony
under the eyes of the Eternal Forgiver, did not expiate the
guilt of all others! The misery of this single one pierces to the
very marrow of my life; and thou art calmly grinning at the
fate of thousands!
MEPHISTOPHELES
Now we are already again at the end of our wits, where the
understanding of you men runs wild. Why didst thou enter
into fellowship with us, if thou canst not carry it out? Wilt fly,
and art not secure against dizziness? Did we thrust ourselves
upon thee, or thou thyself upon us?

FAUST

Gnash not thus thy devouring teeth at me? It fills me with
horrible disgust. Mighty, glorious Spirit, who hast vouchsafed
to me Thine apparition, who knowest my heart and my soul,
why fetter me to the felon-comrade, who feeds on mischief and
gluts himself with ruin?

MEPHISTOPHELES

Hast thou done?

FAUST

Rescue her, or woe to thee! The fearfullest curse be upon
thee for thousands of ages!

MEPHISTOPHELES

I cannot loosen the bonds of the Avenger, nor undo his bolts.
Rescue her? Who was it that plunged her into ruin? I, or thou?
(FAUST looks around wildly.)
Wilt thou grasp the thunder? Well that it has not been
given to you, miserable mortals! To crush to pieces the innocent
respondent—that is the tyrant-fashion of relieving one's
self in embarrassments.

FAUST

Take me thither! She shall be free!

MEPHISTOPHELES

And the danger to which thou wilt expose thyself? Know
that the guilt of blood, from thy hand, still lies upon the town!
Avenging spirits hover over the spot where the victim fell, and
lie in wait for the returning murderer.

FAUST

That, too, from thee? Murder and death of a world upon
thee, monster! Take me thither, I say, and liberate her!

MEPHISTOPHELES

I will convey thee there; and hear, what I can do! Have I
all the power in Heaven and on Earth? I will becloud the
jailer's senses: get possession of the key, and lead her forth with
human hand! I will keep watch: the magic steeds are ready,
I will carry you off. So much is in my power.

FAUST

Up and away!

XXIV
NIGHT
OPEN FIELD
(FAUST and MEPHISTOPHELES speeding onward on black horses.)

FAUST
What weave they there round the raven-stone?
MEPHISTOPHELES
I know not what they are brewing and doing.
FAUST
Soaring up, sweeping down, bowing and bending!
MEPHISTOPHELES
A witches'-guild.
FAUST
They scatter, devote and doom!
MEPHISTOPHELES
On! on!
  Dungeon
XXV
DUNGEON
FAUST
(with a bunch of keys and a lamp, before an iron door)
A shudder, long unfelt, comes o'er me;
Mankind's collected woe o'erwhelms me, here.
She dwells within the dark, damp walls before me,
And all her crime was a delusion dear!
What! I delay to free her?
I dread, once again to see her?
On! my shrinking but lingers Death more near.
(He grasps the lock: the sound of singing is heard inside.)
My mother, the harlot,
Who put me to death;
My father, the varlet,
Who eaten me hath!
Little sister, so good,
Laid my bones in the wood,
In the damp moss and clay:
Then was I a beautiful bird o' the wood;
Fly away! Fly away!
FAUST (unlocking)
She does not dream her lover listens near;
That he the rattling chain, the rustling straw, can hear.
(He enters.)

MARGARET (hiding herself on the pallet)
Woe! woe! They come. O death of bitterness!
FAUST (whispering)
Hush! hush! The hour is come that frees thee.
MARGARET (throwing herself before him)
Art thou a man, then pity my distress!
FAUST
Thy cries will wake the guards, and they will seize thee!
(He takes hold of the fetters to unlock them.)
MARGARET (on her knees)
Who, headsman! unto thee such power
Over me could give?
Thou'rt come for me at midnight-hour:
Have mercy on me, let me live!
Is't not soon enough when morning chime has run?
(She rises.)
And I am yet so young, so young!
And now Death comes, and ruin!
I, too, was fair, and that was my undoing.
My love was near, but now he's far;
Torn lies the wreath, scattered the blossoms are.
Seize me not thus so violently!
Spare me! What have I done to thee?
Let me not vainly entreat thee!
I never chanced, in all my days, to meet thee!
FAUST
Shall I outlive this misery?
MARGARET
Now am I wholly in thy might.
But let me suckle, first, my baby!
I blissed it all this livelong night;
They took 't away, to vex me, maybe,
And now they say I killed the child outright.
And never shall I be glad again.
They sing songs about me! 'tis bad of the folk to do it!
There's an old story has the same refrain;
Who bade them so construe it?
FAUST (falling upon his knees)
Here lieth one who loves thee ever,
The thraldom of thy woe to sever.
MARGARET (flinging herself beside him)
O let us kneel, and call the Saints to hide us!
Under the steps beside us,
The threshold under,

Hell heaves in thunder!
The Evil One
With terrible wrath
Seeketh a path
His prey to discover!
FAUST (aloud)
Margaret! Margaret!
MARGARET (attentively listening)
That was the voice of my lover!
(She springs to her feet: the fetters fall off.)
Where is he? I heard him call me.
I am free! No one shall enthrall me.
To his neck will I fly,
On his bosom lie!
On the threshold he stood, and Margaret! calling,
Midst of Hell's howling and noises appalling,
Midst of the wrathful, infernal derision,
I knew the sweet sound of the voice of the vision!
FAUST
'Tis I!
MARGARET
'Tis thou! O, say it once again!
(Clasping him.)
'Tis he! 'tis he! Where now is all my pain?
The anguish of the dungeon, and the chain?
'Tis thou! Thou comest to save me,
And I am saved!—
Again the street I see
Where first I looked on thee;
And the garden, brightly blooming,
Where I and Martha wait thy coming.
FAUST (struggling to leave)
Come! Come with me!
MARGARET
Delay, now!
So fain I stay, when thou delayest!
(Caressing him.)
FAUST
Away, now!
If longer here thou stayest,
We shall be made to dearly rue it.
MARGARET
Kiss me!—canst no longer do it?
My friend, so short a time thou'rt missing,

And hast unlearned thy kissing?
Why is my heart so anxious, on thy breast?
Where once a heaven thy glances did create me,
A heaven thy loving words expressed,
And thou didst kiss, as thou wouldst suffocate me—
Kiss me!
Or I'll kiss thee!
(She embraces him.)
Ah, woe! thy lips are chill,
And still.
How changed in fashion
Thy passion!
Who has done me this ill?
(She turns away from him.)
FAUST
Come, follow me! My darling, be more bold:
I'll clasp thee, soon, with warmth a thousand-fold;
But follow now! 'Tis all I beg of thee.
MARGARET (turning to him)
And is it thou? Thou, surely, certainly?
FAUST
'Tis I! Come on!
MARGARET
Thou wilt unloose my chain,
And in thy lap wilt take me once again.
How comes it that thou dost not shrink from me?—
Say, dost thou know, my friend, whom thou mak'st free?
FAUST
Come! come! The night already vanisheth.
MARGARET
My mother have I put to death;
I've drowned the baby born to thee.
Was it not given to thee and me?
Thee, too!—'Tis thou! It scarcely true doth seem—
Give me thy hand! 'Tis not a dream!
Thy dear, dear hand!—But, ah, 'tis wet!
Why, wipe it off! Methinks that yet
There's blood thereon.
Ah, God! what hast thou done?
Nay, sheathe thy sword at last!
Do not affray me!
FAUST
O, let the past be past!
Thy words will slay me!

MARGARET

No, no! Thou must outlive us.
Now I'll tell thee the graves to give us:
Thou must begin to-morrow
The work of sorrow!
The best place give to my mother,
Then close at her side my brother,
And me a little away,
But not too very far, I pray!
And here, on my right breast, my baby lay!
Nobody else will lie beside me!—
Ah, within thine arms to hide me,
That was a sweet and a gracious bliss,
But no more, no more can I attain it!
I would force myself on thee and constrain it,
And it seems thou repellest my kiss:
And yet 'tis thou, so good, so kind to see!

FAUST

If thou feel'st it is I, then come with me!

MARGARET

Out yonder?

FAUST

To freedom.

MARGARET

If the grave is there,
Death lying in wait, then come!
From here to eternal rest:
No further step—no, no!
Thou goest away! O Henry, if I could go!

FAUST

Thou canst! Just will it! Open stands the door.

MARGARET

I dare not go: there's no hope any more.
Why should I fly? They'll still my steps waylay!
It is so wretched, forced to beg my living,
And a bad conscience sharper misery giving!
It is so wretched, to be strange, forsaken,
And I'd still be followed and taken!

FAUST

I'll stay with thee.

MARGARET

Be quick! Be quick!
Save thy perishing child!
Away! Follow the ridge

Up by the brook,
 If the grave is there, Death lying in wait, then come!
If the grave is there, Death lying in wait, then come!
Over the bridge,
Into the wood,
To the left, where the plank is placed
In the pool!
Seize it in haste!
'Tis trying to rise,
'Tis struggling still!
Save it! Save it!

FAUST

Recall thy wandering will!
One step, and thou art free at last!

MARGARET

If the mountain we had only passed!
There sits my mother upon a stone,—
I feel an icy shiver!
There sits my mother upon a stone,
And her head is wagging ever.
She beckons, she nods not, her heavy head falls o'er;
She slept so long that she wakes no more.
She slept, while we were caressing:
Ah, those were the days of blessing!

FAUST

Here words and prayers are nothing worth;
I'll venture, then, to bear thee forth.

MARGARET

No—let me go! I'll suffer no force!
Grasp me not so murderously!
I've done, else, all things for the love of thee.

FAUST

The day dawns: Dearest! Dearest!

MARGARET

Day? Yes, the day comes,—the last day breaks for me!
My wedding-day it was to be!
Tell no one thou has been with Margaret!
Woe for my garland! The chances
Are over—'tis all in vain!
We shall meet once again,
But not at the dances!
The crowd is thronging, no word is spoken:
The square below
And the streets overflow:

The death-bell tolls, the wand is broken.
I am seized, and bound, and delivered—
Shoved to the block—they give the sign!
Now over each neck has quivered
The blade that is quivering over mine.
Dumb lies the world like the grave!
FAUST
O had I ne'er been born!
MEPHISTOPHELES (appears outside)
Off! or you're lost ere morn.
Useless talking, delaying and praying!
My horses are neighing:
The morning twilight is near.
MARGARET
What rises up from the threshold here?
He! he! suffer him not!
What does he want in this holy spot?
He seeks me!
FAUST
Thou shalt live.
MARGARET
Judgment of God! myself to thee I give.
MEPHISTOPHELES (to FAUST)
Come! or I'll leave her in the lurch, and thee!
MARGARET
Thine am I, Father! rescue me!
Ye angels, holy cohorts, guard me,
Camp around, and from evil ward me!
Henry! I shudder to think of thee.
MEPHISTOPHELES
She is judged!
VOICE (from above)
She is saved!
MEPHISTOPHELES (to FAUST)
Hither to me!
(He disappears with FAUST.)
VOICE (from within, dying away)
Henry! Henry!

Made in the USA
San Bernardino, CA
10 March 2015